"You must be wishing you hadn't seen me at the airport," Camille said.

He gave a tight smile. "It's been an interesting couple of hours." Then he asked, "Can I make you a coffee?"

He'd do that for her when he was still so rattled by her news? She'd thought he'd want to keep aloof while they got down to business. Yet somehow he'd understood her distress, which was more than she did right now. She was all over the place with her feelings about Etienne, Elyna, coming home, everything. "Coffee would be lovely, thanks."

"I think a certain little girl wants to go down." There was a look of need in his eyes, as though he really wanted Elyna to be his daughter.

He was as vulnerable as she was, Camille realized with a shock. Everyone thought the world of Doctor Etienne Laval, but no one ever got behind his barriers. Not even her when they were between the sheets, naked as the day they were born, being physically intimate and yet mentally separate.

Dear Reader,

There's nothing quite so wonderful as setting a story in Paris. As I write, I can image the sights and sounds that I fell in love with when we visited a while ago.

When Camille returns to Paris from Montreal with her baby daughter, she is on a mission. To tell Etienne he is her daughter's father. She knows he won't accept the news well, maybe not at all, but she believes he deserves to know as much as their daughter deserves a loving, caring father. Which Etienne will be if he accepts his role. When Camille broke off their fling a year and a half ago, Etienne was shocked. No woman had ever done that to him before. Can he see beyond his annoyance with the wonderful woman and accept what she tells him about the little girl is true? It goes against his ingrained need to protect his heart to admit he wants nothing more than to open up to Camille. Can he do it? And will Camille, with her own trust issues, accept him into her life?

I enjoyed writing these two's story and hope you enjoy reading it as much.

All the best,

Sue Mackay
suemackayauthor@gmail.com

PARISIAN SURGEON'S SECRET CHILD

SUE MacKAY

Harlequin
MEDICAL ROMANCE

If you purchased this book without a cover you should be aware that this book is stolen property. It was reported as "unsold and destroyed" to the publisher, and neither the author nor the publisher has received any payment for this "stripped book."

Harlequin®
MEDICAL ROMANCE

ISBN-13: 978-1-335-99328-1

Parisian Surgeon's Secret Child

Copyright © 2025 by Sue MacKay

All rights reserved. No part of this book may be used or reproduced in any manner whatsoever without written permission.

Without limiting the author's and publisher's exclusive rights, any unauthorized use of this publication to train generative artificial intelligence (AI) technologies is expressly prohibited.

This is a work of fiction. Names, characters, places and incidents are either the product of the author's imagination or are used fictitiously. Any resemblance to actual persons, living or dead, businesses, companies, events or locales is entirely coincidental.

For questions and comments about the quality of this book, please contact us at CustomerService@Harlequin.com.

TM and ® are trademarks of Harlequin Enterprises ULC.

Harlequin Enterprises ULC	HarperCollins Publishers
22 Adelaide St. West, 41st Floor	Macken House, 39/40 Mayor Street Upper,
Toronto, Ontario M5H 4E3, Canada	Dublin 1, D01 C9W8, Ireland
www.Harlequin.com	www.HarperCollins.com

Printed in U.S.A.

Sue MacKay lives with her husband in New Zealand's beautiful Marlborough Sounds, with the water on her doorstep and the birds and the trees at her back door. It is the perfect setting to indulge her passions of entertaining friends by cooking them sumptuous meals, drinking fabulous wine, going for hill walks or kayaking around the bay—and, of course, writing stories.

Books by Sue MacKay

Harlequin Medical Romance

Queenstown Search & Rescue

Captivated by Her Runaway Doc
A Single Dad to Rescue Her
From Best Friends to I Do?

Stranded with the Paramedic
Single Mom's New Year Wish
Brought Together by a Pup
Fake Fiancée to Forever?
Resisting the Pregnant Pediatrician
Marriage Reunion with the Island Doc
Paramedic's Fling to Forever
Healing the Single Dad Surgeon
Brooding Vet for the Wallflower
Wedding Date with the ER Doctor

Visit the Author Profile page
at Harlequin.com for more titles.

**Praise for
Sue MacKay**

"Ms. MacKay has delivered a really good read in this book where the chemistry between this couple was strong; the romance was delightful and had me loving how these two come together."
—*Harlequin Junkie* on *The Italian Surgeon's Secret Baby*

PROLOGUE

IN THE SURGICAL ward at Paris Central Hospital Nurse Camille Beauregard looked around while she waited as general surgeon Etienne Laval filled in another nurse on a patient he'd operated on that afternoon. Something didn't feel quite right.

On the opposite side of the four-bed room they stood outside, a post-op patient lay overly still, her chest barely rising or falling. Her hands were spread wide and tight on her abdomen.

Camille raced across. 'Hello?'

'Camille? What's up?' Etienne called after her.

'Something's wrong.' The woman's face was grey and glistened with sweat. 'Hello, can you hear me?' Reaching for the patient's wrist, Camille found a weak, slow pulse. She slammed the emergency buzzer at the same time calling to the nurse Etienne had been talking to. 'Amelie, get the defib. Now.'

'Cardiac arrest?' asked Etienne, already at the other side of the bed with his interlaced hands close to the woman's chest, ready to do compressions as he checked over what he could see.

'Not yet. I'm being prepared because I believe it's going to happen.' *Please keep beating, heart*, she pleaded in her head.

Then they were surrounded with nurses and a trolley of emergency equipment.

She reached for the defibrillator, still certain the situation was about to deteriorate.

'Prepare the defibrillator,' Etienne commanded as he tore open the hospital gown covering the woman's chest.

'Onto it.' Camille had the defib pads in hand and immediately put them in place. 'Get the machine up to speed, Amelie. We might not need it but time is of the essence if we do.' Deep down she knew what was coming.

'Yes, it's happening. Now,' Etienne cut in. 'Stand back,' he continued when the defib beeped. It was ready.

Camille held her breath as the current lifted the woman partially off the mattress. As she fell back the line on the defib screen rose, fell, rose and fell. 'Phew, that was close.' *Thank you, heart.* Her own heart was beating wildly. Sometimes this work could be too much.

'Agreed.' The relief was also obvious in Etienne's voice. 'Whose patient is she?' he asked, his gaze totally focused on the heart monitor where the green line moved up and down.

'Beau's,' the head nurse, Karina, told him. 'She came up from Theatre about an hour ago. Amelie's her nurse.'

'There were no signs of anything wrong with her heart. I checked often.' Amelie sounded defensive. 'It's all there in the notes.'

Camille gave her a quick smile. 'It's all right. These things happen sometimes, Amelie.'

As the head nurse took over monitoring the woman Etienne stepped back. 'I'll call Beau to let him know what's happened.'

'Thanks, Etienne,' Karina replied. 'Pass the phone over when you're done. I need to ask him a few things.'

With nothing else for her to do, Camille went to check on one of her patients in another room along the corridor. Her hands shook as she thought about what might've happened if she hadn't sensed something was wrong. Sometimes instinct was a game changer, but that was the first time hers had kicked in quite like that, something to be grateful for. Odd how shaken she felt. It wasn't as though emergencies didn't arise with post-op patients. Thankfully there were less than two hours to go before she was off duty and out of here on three months' leave. It was hard to believe how uptight she was. But then emotionally she was all over the place what with heading away to Montreal in two days' time, and another, bigger issue to contend with.

'Camille. Wait.'

Her heart sank. The very man she was going to talk to later and change his world for ever, along with hers, stood beside her and she hadn't even seen him coming. Hadn't sensed his presence. For her telling him her news was going to be as drastic as saving that woman's life. Difficult was another word for what had to be said. Lifting her head slowly, she faced Etienne. 'Yes?' Why did he have to look so hot? To fill her head with memories of getting as close as humanly possible to that amazing body? Reminding her of a need for more of the pleasure he'd induced in her?

'You were brilliant. How did you know she was in trouble?' Wonder shone in his eyes.

For a brief moment she felt all tender inside. 'Instinct, I guess.' She shrugged. What else could she say when she didn't fully understand what had gone down either? 'I sensed there was a problem.'

'And leapt in to deal with it. Well done.' He touched her shoulder lightly.

Highly out of order on the ward, but no one was around to see. And right now, with what she had to tell him later, she wasn't about to make a fuss. Unfortunately there was no denying the heat that casual touch created within her. A heat that had already led to a one-night stand after a staff party where she'd seen a different, sexier side to surgeon Laval and been instantly attracted to him. The one night together hadn't been enough and they'd continued to indulge their passion for more incredible nights over the following weeks until she'd begun to think she might be getting too involved and called a halt to the fling. *If only it were that simple.* 'Thank you.'

Turning, she headed down the ward, checking her watch and ignoring the thumping under her ribs. *She* wasn't having a cardiac arrest, merely stressing about how to deal with the conversation yet to come. Etienne would not take her news lightly. More than likely he wouldn't believe it, but that was no excuse not to tell him. She'd put it off until now because she had to work alongside him on the ward until she left for Montreal. Having him give her the cold shoulder because he might not accept her news would be hell. He'd been ultra careful about using protection. She'd been sceptical when she'd first realised she'd missed a period, but blood tests didn't lie.

Etienne had the right to know she was pregnant. She wanted him to know. Her child was not going to grow up as she had, always wondering who his father was, where he was, why he didn't love him when he hadn't even met him. Her hand touched her tummy. Twelve weeks. She was certain it was a boy in there. There was no reason behind that, just a feeling she was right. And look how well her instincts had played out for the woman recovering from abdominal surgery minutes ago.

The fling with Etienne had been amazing, unlike any she'd had before. So good that he'd begun sneaking into her head when she wasn't looking, even tapping on her heart, which was why she'd pulled the plug—much to his amazement. Apparently women didn't ever do that to Etienne Laval. His reputation went before him. He was open to short flings, nothing else, and he decided when they were over. By all accounts the women he slept with usually hung around for all they could get. He was single, wealthy beyond comprehension, and incredibly handsome. No doubt a great catch in some people's books. He would be in hers too if love were possible, but it wasn't. She wasn't seeking financial help from him, and, frankly, that was about all he could offer because she doubted that, with the way his emotions remained untouchable except in bed, he was available for love any more than she was.

Her heart had been smashed once when she'd trusted the wrong man. She wasn't falling for Etienne when he wasn't into anything deep and meaningful. But she would tell him the truth and hope they could work together amicably over raising their child when she returned to Paris. She instinctively crossed her fingers, knowing what a long shot that was. Telling Etienne tonight would give him time to accept the situation and think about how they managed parenthood when they weren't in a relationship. She would raise her child, but also wanted Etienne to be a part of his upbringing, just not a part of her personal life.

She'd be back from Montreal before the birth and then they could sit down and work out everything in a way that suited all three of them.

Two hours later Camille drew a deep breath and stepped purposefully up to the partially open door of Etienne's office, then stopped.

She could see through the gap that he was sitting in his chair with his feet on the desk, a phone to his ear, looking good enough to eat and reminding her how wonderful making love with him had been. She should call what they'd got up to sex, not lovemaking, and keep it in line with not wanting to get too involved, but it wasn't easy. There'd been something about Etienne that ignored her need to remain as protective of her heart as she usually was.

'No, Mum, I will not take Beatrice to the ball. She's completely focused on marrying me when we aren't even in a relationship and that's the last thing I ever intend doing.'

Silence ensued as he listened to his mother.

Camille knew she should knock on the door to let him know she was here. It wouldn't help her case if he caught her eavesdropping on a personal conversation. Or ogling that tight, sexy body of his, which should be the last thing on her mind. Etienne could be a big distraction when she didn't have her sensible hat on. Raising her hand, she paused as he continued talking.

'She's already tried the "she loves me" approach.' The fingers of one hand flicked in the air as he spoke. 'I'm so over what women come up with to try and move in with me, or get a marriage proposal. The only lie I haven't encountered in a while is the fake pregnancy one, and I bet it's not far away again. Yes, I am a cynic, and you know why. I expect women to lie to me, not be honest. I will not take Beatrice to the ball.'

Camille's shoulders sagged. She immediately straightened up. She was tempted to get out of here. Etienne had just given her the best possible reason to keep her mouth shut, except she didn't want to do that. She couldn't. It wouldn't be right for any of them. If only there were a chance he wouldn't automatically disbelieve that she was pregnant, and thereby refuse to accept he was the father. Her own father had left before she came into the world, not to be seen until he wanted something from her.

Basically Etienne had just proved her suspicions right about how he'd react to her news. However, he *was* her baby's father and therefore deserved to know just as her child deserved to have a father in his life. She wasn't about to demand she move in with him, she only wanted him aware of his parenthood, but his barriers were already up and she hadn't even uttered a word. No surprise there. He was always friendly but never once, even when he appeared completely relaxed, had she been able to see past that to what lay behind his handsome face.

Time to face the music. Her heart was heavy. She knew what it was like to grow up without meeting her father until she was twenty and then ruing the years she'd wasted wondering who he might be and longing to know him, along with cursing her mother for not telling Grandma and Grandpa who he was before she died. At least *her* child had a decent man for a father despite his issues about what women expected from him.

Etienne was still talking. 'You also know why I never intend becoming a parent.'

He didn't even want children? Didn't want to be a father? That was altogether different. She *was* out of here. Etienne was not going to know he was already on the way to becoming a parent. Not now, probably never. Make that definitely never. Her blood was suddenly boiling. Her child wasn't going to know the same pain she had because of her father. She turned away.

'Camille, what are you doing here?'

She swore under her breath. He'd spotted her. What could she say to that? Especially since his mother would no doubt hear whatever came out of her mouth? Their brief fling had ended abruptly because she'd known she was starting to fall for Etienne. Hoping to get into a serious relationship with this man was like believing her phone never needed its battery charged up. If she'd even been looking for a long-term connection he wasn't her type, which didn't help her to understand why she'd begun falling for him in the first place. Like her, he didn't do serious relationships, or so he'd told her the very first time they'd slept together. Not that there'd been any sleeping going on. She pushed the door open fully. 'Nothing important.' Only the most important thing in her life at the moment.

'Just a minute, Mum. I have an idea. Camille, would you go as my partner to a charity ball my mother's organising?'

'No, thank you. I'm busy that week.'

His face froze. Of course he wasn't used to being turned down. He gave a deliberate shrug as if to say he didn't care what she said. 'I haven't told you when it's being held.'

'I don't do balls.' Not true. She loved dancing but he wasn't to know that.

'Really?' He was looking at her as if she'd lost her mind.

She probably had, but there was a bigger problem between them. Even if she weren't heading to Canada, going anywhere with him was off the cards until he knew about her pregnancy and then he'd no longer ask her to accompany him to a coffee break on the ward if she was still working there. He'd been away at a conference until today and obviously hadn't heard this was her last day for a while. Anyway, she was not prepared to go through the pain of being made to look like a selfish, lying woman who had obviously schemed and connived to get what she wanted from him. Coming here was turning out to be a huge mistake. She managed a shrug of her own. 'Really. I'm off home now, so carry on talking to your mother.' She turned to leave.

'Wait. Why *did* you drop by?'

The only lie I haven't encountered in a while is the fake pregnancy one.

'It's all right. I made a mistake.' One she did not want to accept. For all the wrong reasons in this case, Etienne expected someone to tell him that he'd unwittingly fathered a child because he'd been lied to about it before. He deserved to know it was true in her case, and then make some decisions, but not right now, when she was so angry and upset. She'd be back in Paris well before her baby arrived. She might talk to him then. It could be easier to do once she'd spent a few months thinking through what she'd heard and how to make it work for everyone. But right now she couldn't see herself ever telling him.

A sudden sense of loss took over from all the other emotions simmering through her, forcing her to turn and look at him one last time. It might've been a fling, but there'd been something warm and special about their short time together, despite how Etienne hid behind a façade he thought no one saw—more reason why she'd walked away with her heart intact while she still could. And now she was carrying *their* baby.

'Goodbye, Etienne,' she said softly.

Going to Montreal with her grandmother was a trip that had been a long time coming. Her grandfather grew up there and moved to Paris when he met Grandma, who was Parisian through and through. He wanted his ashes taken to Montreal when he died to be buried alongside his parents. She couldn't pull out without letting Grandma down, and that wasn't happening no matter what else was going on in her life. Not after everything her grandparents had done for her from the day she was born.

Inexplicably her eyes blurred with tears as she made her way to the elevator. Deep down she mightn't believe Etienne was really her type but there was no denying he was a wonderful man and that she did have strong feelings for him. She'd got herself into a right mess getting pregnant. So much for taking every precaution available. Something had failed. Now she had a number of serious problems to sort and whichever way she went someone was going to get hurt. If only Etienne were easier to approach, other than when going to bed with him, but he wasn't. Unfortunately she would never trust any man, wonderful or not, with her heart after the one she had loved and believed she'd spend her life with, Benoit, had forgotten to mention the wife and two daughters he lived with. Never again would she give her heart away. It was too painful when everything went belly up.

Etienne wondered what he'd done wrong for Camille to react as though he'd asked her to go to a hanging. It was refreshing on one level, he had to admit. Also rare. It also sucked. He actually liked more about her than just the awesome sex they'd shared during their fling. Their first time together had come about because she'd looked so sexy in a short skirt and tight top accentuating her perfect figure, something he'd only guessed at before as she was always in scrubs at work. To his surprise she hadn't tried everything possible to get more than a few nights between the sheets.

She'd snuck under his radar when he'd thought he was invincible. Worse, it had been Camille who'd finished their time together, not him. A totally new experience for him. 'When was I last turned down for any invitation?'

'Seems to me she could be a keeper.'

Etienne groaned. He'd forgotten about his mother being on the other end of the phone. Camille was a distraction when he wasn't being careful. 'Come on, that's excessive.' In his book there was no such thing as a woman being a keeper. Yes, he was a cynic, but after being hurt once, twice wasn't happening. 'I'll go on my own to the ball. It's not as though I won't get to dance with women who aren't already hooked up with a man.'

There were always females attending without partners for various reasons. Besides, while he was happy to take to the dance floor, it wasn't essential. He'd do his bit at the auction to raise funds for a children's charity, catch up with people he knew, and then maybe get an early night for a change. Life had become boring, he decided. Safer but dull as cold fries. Which did not mean he was going to step beyond the firm barriers he kept around his heart. Nor was he going to have a family. Not after going through the agony of losing his brother and watching his parents struggle to deal with their pain while supporting his sister and him. It had been so hard for all of them.

'Who is this woman? Did you call her Camille?' Of course, she knew the answer to that. His mother had a habit of stirring when it came to his lack of a love life. She refused to accept that because his first and only serious girlfriend had wrecked his belief in true love, he wasn't interested in finding another woman to try again. She probably had a point. He did get lonely at times, but not enough to go through pain like Melina had caused him.

Melina had opened his eyes completely, never to be closed again. Only weeks before they were due to marry he'd overheard her talking to a friend about how relieved she'd be for all the fuss to be over so she could get back to focusing on her own plans for the future. She'd said she'd do everything required to help Etienne and his family with their many business and charity commitments so no one thought she was there only for the lifestyle, even if that was why she was marrying him.

When he'd questioned if she'd loved him at all Melina had said love wasn't all it was cracked up to be and that working together on projects was more important. Basically she was all about herself, and not a lot for him. It had shocked him to the core to hear her say that love wasn't important. Hence he'd cancelled the wedding only for her to tell him he couldn't because she was pregnant with his child. That had been a desperate lie. There was no baby. He hadn't spoken to her since. What he'd struggled with most was that deep down he'd regretted there not being a baby despite believing he didn't want to be a parent. He'd begun to accept he was going to be a father and then it was torn away from him; a reminder of why he wanted to avoid parenthood.

'Etienne? You're not answering me,' said his mother.

'Camille's a nurse on the surgical ward.' A very

caring, firm but sympathetic nurse whom patients adored, and doctors appreciated. A nurse whose instincts were off the planet after what he'd witnessed today. Camille calling off their fling had been a novelty, one he hadn't quite managed to put behind him. Something he admired and that kept him aware of her far too much.

'Sounding better by the minute,' chuckled his mother.

'Time I checked up on a patient. Talk during the weekend.' He hung up before Mum could add any more pointless comments to the conversation. Camille had turned him down so he'd go alone to the function. Say no more.

It never failed to amaze him how women believed they only had to be exceptional in bed to get a free ride into his life full-time. No wonder he wouldn't be rushing to the altar any time soon. More likely never. To think he'd loved Melina like no one else. When they'd first met he'd fallen hard and fast, and had never wanted to be without her at his side.

He hadn't trusted another woman with his heart since, and doubted he ever would. Just because Camille Beauregard didn't swoon at his feet didn't mean she wouldn't be out to get what she wanted from him either. Yep, he was definitely a cynic, but that was what kept him safe. Wasn't it?

CHAPTER ONE

As THE WHEELS touched down on the runway at Charles de Gaulle Airport Camille grinned with excitement and relief. She was finally home after fifteen months in Montreal. A tumultuous and heartbreaking period of her life along with some of the most wonderful moments to lift her spirits. She was ready to do the decent thing and introduce her wee daughter to her father no matter what he said or thought. She'd been wrong about having a boy, and couldn't care less. Elyna was her adorable girl.

She was as ready as she'd ever be considering that Etienne wouldn't be easy to confront, would be looking for reasons not to believe her because apparently every woman wanted something from him and would go to any length to get it. But it had to be done for her daughter's sake if not Etienne's, and she wouldn't put it off any longer.

She'd let Etienne down by not stepping up and telling him before she left for Canada. The fact she'd heard him saying he'd never believe a woman who told him she was having his baby was irrelevant. That he didn't intend being a parent was different, but she owed him the opportunity to rethink that. Guilt had weighed heavily on her from the day she'd held Elyna in her arms for the first time. It had been a very brief moment before the doctors had taken her daughter away to Paediatric Intensive Care where she'd spent weeks in an incubator. Being born eight weeks premature hadn't given her the best start but she'd made up for it ever since, growing fast and being so cheerful and alert to everything going on around her. Elyna was amazing.

As she turned to her sleeping daughter tucked firmly in a child seat with a pink blanket wrapped around her, Camille's grin slowly faded. Etienne might want nothing to do with his child, or he might demand more than his share of time with her, and want to have all the say in how and where she was raised. He wouldn't. Would he? It just showed how little she really knew the man. Their fling had been amazing but it had been all about the wonderful sex, not spending time getting to know each other on a deeper level.

After the way Benoit had treated her when she'd loved him so much, getting too involved with a man was something she had no intention of doing again. The day a woman had knocked on her door five years ago and introduced herself as Benoit's wife and the mother of his two children

Camille had closed herself off to ever being that vulnerable again. Not only had Benoit broken her heart but he'd shown her she was far too trustful and should never have readily accepted the things he'd told her about himself. But wasn't that what a person did when they loved and trusted someone? Believed them. To check out everything Benoit had said would've undermined their relationship and her feelings for him—and exposed the truth before she got too invested in him.

She fully expected Etienne to refuse to accept Elyna was his daughter because he was already waiting for someone to try that trick again, but it'd still hurt if he thought she could be so selfish and conniving. At least it'd be less likely he'd want to take charge of Elyna's life, but if he did that'd be the worst outcome. They'd be forever fighting over Elyna's parenting and how to raise her, because no matter what ideas Etienne came up with she would always stick by her daughter. Elyna was more important than anyone else in her life.

There lay her biggest fear, because she'd never be able to afford the ongoing legal costs if Etienne did get down and dirty over who raised their child. With his extreme wealth she hadn't a chance. She sighed. She still owed her daughter the chance to know her father, even one who'd said he didn't want children. Elyna needed him in her life so they had to work through this. It wasn't in her to keep Etienne a secret from Elyna. Her own mother had never told anyone who her daughter's father was even when, two days after she gave birth, she knew she was dying from severe septicaemia. Camille didn't want Elyna to know that pain. It had undermined her ability to believe her mother had been a loving person, even when her grandparents had said she was and that she'd adored Camille for the short time she was with her.

But having finally met the man when she was twenty, Camille had finally understood why her mother had kept her father's identity a secret. She hadn't liked him from the moment he'd turned up at her apartment to introduce himself in a smarmy manner, trying to ingratiate himself in her life because he'd missed out on so much due to her mother being a lying bitch. He'd turned out to be only about himself and was a useless piece of work, relying on others to pay his way through life. Why her mother had ever got together with him was beyond Camille's comprehension except for wondering if maybe love really was blind.

At least Elyna didn't have a father like that. He was upright and kind, and could be fun when he wasn't wondering what someone wanted from him, which appeared to be most of the time he wasn't concentrating on patients. But he also wasn't going to immediately believe her when she said Elyna was his.

Camille unclipped her seat belt and glanced around at the disembarking passengers. She'd wait until they'd finished getting their bags down from the overhead lockers and made their way to the front before getting her own gear.

'Do you want a hand with Elyna?' a stewardess asked when the plane was nearly empty. The woman had been a treasure throughout the flight, taking Elyna for a walk up and down the aisle when she got grizzly and feeding her so Camille could enjoy her own meal.

'Thanks, but I'll be fine.' Her little girl was still sound asleep and hopefully would remain so for a while longer, though collecting luggage and going through Immigration would probably wake her. With a bit of luck she wouldn't be too unsettled, but the chances were slim. As good a reason as any for spending money she shouldn't on a taxi instead of catching the train to her apartment where her friend, Liza, had kindly got in supplies for the next couple of days.

Liza had visited her in Montreal when Elyna was two weeks old and had happily accepted the role of surrogate aunt, since Camille had had no close family other than her grandmother who was counting down the time she had left in this world. 'Come on, baby girl. We have a special place to go.' Home. Her home, left to her by her grandparents. Her safe haven.

Important as it was to go and see Etienne to inform him he had a daughter, she wasn't doing that today. If only she'd had his number she'd have talked to him months ago when she'd realised she wouldn't be returning to Paris for a lot longer than first planned but she'd deleted it after overhearing him say he didn't want to be a father. And she'd had no luck with his secretary at the hospital, either.

Before her grandmother had died, she'd talked about Etienne with her and how what he'd said had closed her off to giving him a chance to rethink his stance on fatherhood. Her grandmother's gentle persuasion had made her see he deserved to know regardless, and that there had to be more behind his statement than the fact women lied to him regularly. That wasn't a strong enough reason to never have a family, surely? Finally, Camille had accepted Grandma was right and there was only one way to find out where Etienne stood. For that she had to face him.

Thirty minutes after exiting the plane Camille piloted a trolley laden with bags and Elyna sitting in the carrier space towards the taxi rank. People were pushing and shoving, talking and laughing, shouting and cursing. She was back in Paris. It felt so good to be home.

'Camille? Is that you?'

What? Only Liza knew she was arriving today and she didn't have a deep, husky male voice. Looking around, she tried to find someone she knew.

'Camille, it *is* you.' Etienne Laval appeared in front of her, looking as stunning as she recalled. 'Thought I recognised that mass of blonde hair.' He leaned in and brushed a light kiss over her cheek that set her skin afire. 'Where have you been?'

Etienne. No. Please no. Anyone but Etienne. Not when she had Elyna with her. Her heart sank. So much for getting time to settle in before talking to him. She wasn't ready. Would she ever be? Probably not. But now? At the airport? No way. Elyna came first and any minute now she'd let rip with grizzles, which would not go down well with Etienne or anyone within hearing distance. So far she'd been interested in what was going on around them but that couldn't last much longer.

'I've just flown in from Montreal and am really tired so I need to grab a taxi, if you don't mind.' She was being abrupt but she so wasn't ready to confront him. Already her mind was tossing up the many questions he would ask. Worse, rubbing it in that there was no way he'd ever believe he was Elyna's father. Then again, she had no idea how he'd react if he did believe her and that was harder to cope with, as there were lots of questions she needed answers for. About his role, her role, what he'd want. On and on they went.

His face fell and he took a step back. 'Fine.' Then his gaze dropped to the trolley. More specifically to Elyna. His eyes widened. Then his mouth flattened. 'I see congratulations are in order.'

If only you knew. 'Thank you.'

He looked around, then back at her. 'Did you travel without help?'

'Yes.' As if she had a nanny on hand.

'Then shouldn't someone be picking up you and your precious cargo?'

Ironic to say the least. Her smile was weak. 'I'm on my own.'

'No partner?'

'No.'

His face became devoid of emotion. 'Really?'

'Yes, really.' Suddenly she felt lonely. There was a battle looming and she had to face it on her own. Even Liza wasn't around, having gone off yesterday to Marseilles on her first holiday in over three years.

'Where're you headed? Your daughter will be exhausted too.' Talk about persistent. Something to remember. Though she did know that much about him, she recalled.

'Rue Roy. In the 8th arrondissement. I have an apartment there.'

'I know where it is.' Of course he did. He'd

dropped her off there once during their fling. 'Come on. My driver will give you a lift on the way to my house.' He was looking at Elyna with studied indifference. 'She's cute,' he muttered.

Her lungs went on hold. Would he figure it out? Did he remember the time that she'd dropped into his office and then left without saying why she'd been there? Probably not. She hadn't been that important in his busy life. 'I think so.'

Now Etienne was studying her closely.

A cold shiver ran down her back. He suspected something wasn't right, and when he let that settle in his head there really was only one way to come out the other end. That was not something she was prepared to talk about here. 'Thanks for the offer of a ride but I'll grab a taxi.' The queue was shrinking quickly. She wouldn't have long to wait.

Ignoring her, Etienne pressed an icon on his phone. 'Alain, I'm ready. We've also got two passengers.' The phone returned to his pocket. 'Sorted.' He stepped nearer and took the trolley from her lifeless hands. 'This way.'

This was definitely not the man she'd known. Too abrupt, but then again he was only thinking about what he wanted. *Stop, Camille. That's unfair. Give him a chance to think everything through.* He'd always been considerate as long as she didn't want anything personal from him, and today she'd be giving him the biggest shock possible. Would he believe her? What would he want to do about it if he did? 'Etienne, give me back the trolley. I am not going with you.' She needed to get Elyna to the apartment where she could crawl around letting off steam. 'I mean it.' Getting away from Etienne was a priority.

He started walking along the pavement. 'So do I.'

To think he'd tried to find Camille when she'd first left the hospital. He'd told himself he just wanted to know why she'd come by his office at the end of that day, which he did, but even more he'd realised he longed to catch up with her and pass the time of day. Just as well he hadn't or he'd have looked silly since it seemed she'd moved on with her life pretty fast after their fling. Strange how that was what *he* usually did. Said goodbye to one woman and quickly found the next one willing to keep his sheets warm for a few weeks. Cynic to the fore. Selfish, perhaps. He might be driven to protect himself from falling in love, but surely the time had to come when he might let go a little and try to find someone who mattered more to him than a few rounds of sex?

He instantly glanced sideways. Why did that particular thought arise out of the blue? Camille might have tweaked his interest, but she was a mother now, and she hadn't done that by herself. But she had said she was on her own.

Another glance to take in the beautiful sight dragging her feet beside him. The shadows beneath her eyes didn't detract from the classic features that made Camille look so lovely. Her tangled, long blonde hair still had the power to make his fingers itch with the need to run through the waves that cascaded over her shoulders. Her clothes were casual, no doubt practical when flying long haul with a toddler, but his memory could still picture what the clothing covered, and raise his temperature above normal. No denying Camille had got to him more than any other woman since Melina. Also, no denying he was not open to another fling with Camille, or to getting to know her better in more ways than sexually. Especially now she had a child. And now he was on edge. Something didn't feel right.

Deep down he'd suspected she'd come to tell him something important the night she'd turned up in his office doorway and then walked away again without saying a word. She'd even turned down the chance to go to the ball with him. So unlike other women. She hadn't been one for cornering him and suggesting anything she thought might get attention from him. It had been the thing about her he'd most admired other than her nursing skills and concern for others. For Camille to do that said there had to have been something she'd needed to discuss with him. Then again, he might've been looking for what was usually never there—a genuine friendliness towards him.

He looked at the little tot before him. She was lovely. Not intending to be a father, he wasn't one for getting all soft over babies, but this little girl unexpectedly stirred him. The child was a girl, right? Camille likely wouldn't dress a boy in bright pink. Not the Camille he thought he knew. But how well had he known her? Not very, other than as a nurse and a sensual lover. Then she'd gone and had a baby within a time frame that caught at him, had him wondering the impossible. Surely, he had to be wrong. The child was tiny so the timing didn't fit. Did it? 'How old is your daughter?'

Camille's head shot around and she stared at him. 'Eleven months.'

Then she wasn't his. Relief should be pouring through him, but instead the tension growing since he'd first seen Camille kept increasing. 'She's tiny.'

'She was eight weeks premature.'

Kick him in the guts, why didn't she? But she still hadn't said the girl was his.

A car pulled up at the kerb. Alain. Relief filled Etienne. Though why he should be relieved he had no clue, other than this was a familiar thing to do. He wanted to talk with Camille so he could put his mind at rest about her child, but not here on the pavement at the airport. Nor in the back of his car where Alain might overhear. It had to be a private conversation in a place where no one could interrupt. 'Camille, this is my ride. Please get in. Alain can drop you off at your apartment.' Had he sounded concerned for her in a positive way? He hoped so, because so far he'd been abrupt, and that wouldn't get him anywhere when what he wanted was to find out the truth—though he suspected he might already have an idea about that. But he was getting ahead of himself. He needed to hear it from Camille, first.

Her smile was tight. 'All right. I guess the sooner I get to my apartment, the better. My girl's exhausted and has had enough of sitting in one spot for so long, no doubt thinking I'm a terrible mother for not letting her crawl up and down the aisles in the plane.'

'I can't imagine you're a terrible mother at all.' It was true. She'd be firm but kind and caring. Or so he believed.

Startled eyes met his. 'Thank you again.'

He liked that he'd surprised her. He wasn't the only one feeling out of sorts here, which added to the feeling he might be right about the child being his. 'Do you need supplies for the kitchen?' They could stop at a supermarket on the way. He'd be helpful, if nothing else.

That messy hair that entranced him swung across her shoulders as she replied. 'No, thanks. My friend's organised everything I need for the next few days so I don't have to go anywhere.' Turning away, she placed the portable seat in the back of the car before lifting the toddler from the trolley and brushing a light kiss over her little face, tightening his heart in the process. Then she leaned inside and settled her daughter into the portable seat before attaching the seat belt.

Heat instantly blasted through him. Camille's figure appeared to have filled out slightly, probably due to the pregnancy, and she looked even lovelier. As she reached further to adjust the seat belt, her trousers stretched across her sexy backside, further outlining the curved shape and reminding him of how he'd held her against him, arousing him. Spinning away, he strode to the driver's door. 'Alain, we're going to Rue Roy.'

Whether he'd stay and talk to Camille about these strange thoughts regarding the little girl whose presence was tipping his world sideways was a decision suddenly beyond him. Remembering Camille's sensational body wrapped around him as he slid inside her had brought him out in a sweat and was messing with his mind. Worse, those memories made him want to touch her, feel her satiny skin under his fingertips. That was an absolute no-no. He was not getting intimate with Camille—now or ever again. Especially when he had no idea what was going on. He could not be this child's father. He couldn't. Could he? His heart shifted, making him wonder how he'd feel if he was.

The back door clicked shut as Camille settled herself beside her daughter. He made to go around to the front passenger seat, then stopped. The last thing he was, was a coward. He might be worried about how much seeing Camille again had rattled him, but he was strong. Melina had not taken that away from him, only his ability to fall in love or trust again.

Opening the back door on the other side to Camille, he slid in beside the little girl, who was again staring at him with enormous blue eyes, her thumb in her mouth. She didn't get those eyes from him. They were all Camille. Something like love flickered under his sternum. It couldn't be love. He didn't know this child who probably had nothing to do with him. He hadn't even known she existed until a few minutes ago. But something was pulling at his heart, saying 'look at me', and it wasn't only those eyes. It went deeper— down to the part of himself he never shared. His heart and the longing for love and family, if he could get past his fear of losing a child as his parents had.

Damn it. His hands clenched on his thighs. *Camille, you might just have upturned my life. I don't know what's going on and I don't know if I want to find out.* He might be in real trouble here. He glanced across to Camille, his heart stuttering again, this time at the worry filling her face. He owned some of that for taking charge about giving her a lift to Rue Roy. He had been blindsided, but that didn't mean he had to be an arrogant sod about it. 'Camille, please relax.'

She blinked in surprise but said nothing. Nor did the tension tightening her body diminish.

Sinking back into the leather seat, he stared sightlessly out of the window.

'Where did you fly in from?' Camille eventually asked in a stilted manner.

Turning back, he told her, 'New York. I've been to a general surgeons' conference for discussions on new technology regarding bowel surgeries.'

'Was it useful?'

'Yes, but I think it'll take time to come into full use around the world.'

Etienne couldn't help himself. He looked down at the tot sitting between them. She was still staring at him and now her mouth was puckered up, looking cute. Again there was a lightness in his chest. Could she really be his? Nothing about her seemed familiar. No Laval features, but neither could he see Camille in her face other than those beautiful eyes. 'Who does she look like?'

'My grandmother.'

'Not your own mother?' He knew nothing about Camille's family, in fact knew next to nothing about her at all.

'From photos I've seen I'd say she's a bit like her, *oui*.'

'You don't remember what your mother looked like?'

'I was only two days old when she died.'

Etienne slumped back in his seat. It was time to shut up and stop asking questions if he was only going to get appalling answers. He might want to learn more about her but nothing so dreadful. 'Camille, I don't know what to say. Sorry seems inadequate.'

'And irrelevant,' she replied briefly. 'It's the only life I've known and I was very happy growing up with my grandparents. Also very lucky. They were wonderful.'

She hadn't gone for the sympathy vote in an attempt to get him onside. He appreciated that, and felt a softening towards her. But then it could be exactly what she'd set out to do. Yes, once more he was being cynical, but he'd had enough lessons from grasping women to last him for ever so it was hard to put those aside with Camille, however briefly. It was also very tempting to do just that. There was something special about her that used to catch at him at times when he wasn't being too cautious. Something he had to remain aware of so he didn't get caught out and lose his heart once more. Yet he couldn't keep quiet, feeling compelled to learn more about her.

'What about your father? Where was he when you were growing up?'

'My mother never saw him again after she told him she was pregnant.'

There was a chill in her voice that had him sitting back and looking at her. He suspected he wasn't the only one with trust issues. Did this explain anything about the little girl sitting in between them?

Damn, why had he called out to Camille the moment he saw her at the airport? Feeling pleased to see her meant nothing compared to the confusion and fear building up inside him now. The sooner they reached Rue Roy, the better; he'd be able to go home and get back on track.

Except he already knew that wasn't happening any time soon, if at all.

CHAPTER TWO

SUDDENLY ELYNA BEGAN to cry. She'd had enough of being restrained. Throw in exhaustion and it was no surprise. Camille was only grateful her girl hadn't had a complete meltdown while on the plane. There'd have been daggers in her back from annoyed passengers.

'Hey, sweetheart, we're nearly there.' She rubbed her daughter's head softly as they drove through the familiar streets of home, taking it all in and trying to ignore the tension rippling off Etienne. Whatever his reaction when he learned he was Elyna's father, Camille was thrilled to be here. She'd missed home, especially in the weeks after her grandmother died, and couldn't wait to return to Paris where she belonged.

Unfortunately it hadn't been a matter of packing her bags and getting on a plane. She'd had a funeral to organise, lawyers to talk to, then the interment of Grandma's ashes in the same plot where they'd put her grandfather's nearly fifteen months earlier. There was no way Grandma was going to be interred anywhere but with him. It had taken a few weeks to sort it all out, but she'd got there.

Now here she was, back in Paris. Weird how she and Etienne had bumped into each other at the airport, as if forces outside her control were playing games with her. She'd intended going to see Etienne as soon as she'd settled in to tell him the truth, but the time had arrived sooner than expected and now she had to get on with it. She felt relieved he was about to find out his role in Elyna's life, but equally nervous. He'd think she was lying because she wanted money or a gracious lifestyle from him. Looking at Elyna, she mentally crossed her fingers, hoping he'd at least listen to her. All she asked for was his acknowledgement that he was Elyna's father.

'It's been a long day for you, hasn't it, little one?'

Elyna cried harder.

Delving into her bag, Camille found the milk bottle and slipped the teat into Elyna's mouth. 'There you go.' Chances were she'd shove it aside as the formula was cold, but not a lot could be done to fix that until they reached the apartment. Any minute now, she sighed. So much for going away for three months. It had taken a long time to get home, many months of pain and sadness over her grandmother's illness and inevitable death, but all along Elyna had added sunshine and love to their days, making things a little less heavy despite being so premature.

Elyna. So far she'd managed not to say her daughter's name out loud because when she did all hell would break loose, and she didn't want that happening in the car with Alain in the front. Elyna was Etienne's grandmother's name. It had been a connection to his family, and also one she really liked.

'It must've seemed like for ever for her,' Etienne commented in that reserved manner he used when not wanting to get too involved with someone. Most of the time.

The voice he used with patients, and with her whenever they'd enjoyed an evening together and it was time for him to head home alone.

'It seems like days since we left Canada but I have to say I'm really proud of her for not getting too upset during the flight.'

'Have you been in Montreal ever since you left Central Hospital?'

'Yes. I went with my grandmother for three months as she wanted to spend time with Grandpa's family, but everything went wrong.' She paused, wondering how much to say. 'Anyway, I've finally made it home.'

He studied her intently. Looking for problems that didn't exist? 'You've had a rough time since leaving Paris, haven't you?'

It sounded as though there were other questions behind that one, but she ignored those and went with, 'I was busy with Grandma and my daughter.' *Our daughter, Etienne.*

Relief filled her as Alain pulled up right outside her apartment block.

Staring up at the building, Camille fought not to give in to the sudden threat of tears. It seemed like for ever since she'd left and she'd been waiting to return for so long she'd started to think it might never happen. When her grandmother had become ill there was no way she'd ever have let her suffer without being there to look after her, even though she also had two nephews living there. Bringing her grandmother back to Paris hadn't been feasible either. Medically Grandma had been diagnosed with heart failure but Camille knew it was more likely a broken heart that took her. She'd missed Grandpa so much over the three years since he'd died that she'd never again been the vibrant lady Camille had known all her life.

'Are you all right?' Etienne asked from outside the car where he stood holding the door open, looking expectantly at her.

What *was* he thinking? He kept looking at Elyna as if he suspected the truth, but that could be her own wishful thinking. 'I'm fine.' She concentrated on extricating Elyna from the car seat. The last thing she wanted was Etienne noticing how upset she was. He might take advantage when she was dreading the discussion they were about to have. 'Hey, baby girl, we're home. You don't have to be buckled in for much longer.' Holding Elyna close, she clambered out of the car.

'Alain, can you give me a hand with Camille's bags? Want to use the pram, Camille?'

'Please.' At the moment when her body ached with exhaustion the thought of carrying Elyna even the small distance to the elevator and up to the apartment seemed too much. 'I'll open it.'

'I do know how to use a pram,' Etienne informed her. 'I have two young nephews whom I've spent plenty of time with.'

So Elyna had cousins. That could be good going forward. 'How old are they?'

'Jacques is five, and Michel is three,' he told her as he set the pram in front of her. 'Here you go.'

Placing Elyna into it, Camille shivered at the cry of annoyance her daughter made. 'Nearly there, sweetheart. Just a few more minutes and you'll be free to explore your new home.' *I promise we're not going anywhere for the next couple of days if it means you have to be restricted.* Though it would be wonderful to stroll along the streets and breathe in Paris, she couldn't buckle Elyna into the pram or a seat anywhere for a while after the long flight they'd endured.

'Lead on,' Etienne called over Elyna's grizzles.

Not bothering to reply, she headed to the main

entrance and tapped in the access code for the building. Liza had given her the up-to-date code in her last email. It might be an old building but it had the modern features that made keys a thing of the past and life a little easier.

The elevator rose to the third floor and the doors whooshed open. For a moment Camille didn't move, simply stood fixed to the floor. She was home, about to start a new chapter of her life, and she wasn't certain how that was going to unfold, which it would start doing the moment she stepped into the apartment she'd grown up in and inherited from her grandparents.

Etienne peered at her. 'Camille?'

Lifting her head high, she stepped out, pushing the pram as she strode along to open the door and go inside, followed by the men with her bags. On the oak sideboard was a vase filled with roses and a card saying 'Welcome Home' leaning against it, no doubt from Liza. Her heart expanded as she walked through to the lounge with the kitchen and dining area to one side.

Stopping in the middle of the large room, she slowly pivoted, taking in the family photos on the walls and on top of an oak cabinet, the rows of well-read books on the shelves, the couch she'd often lain on while watching TV, the view out of the windows of familiar buildings on the opposite side of Rue Roy. She could see and hear, smell and feel her grandparents. They were here. This was a part of them, where they'd raised her, loved her, given her a wonderful life. The tasty family meals eaten at that table, the discussions they'd had in this room about her career, schoolwork, boyfriends. The arguments about wearing make-up when she was only twelve, and what she was wearing to go to the movies with her girlfriends.

'Camille, what's up? Are you all right?' Etienne was looking up at her from where he'd crouched to release the strap holding Elyna in the pram.

No, she wasn't all right. She was overwhelmed. She hadn't expected these emotions to blindside her. It had been over six years since she'd moved out to share a pokey apartment with Liza but she'd thought she was coming back to the one place she loved most to get on with life, not to have so many memories flood her and make her sadder than she'd been at her grandmother's funeral.

Etienne stood in front of her, his hands on her shoulders. 'Camille, don't cry.'

She hadn't known she was. Using her forearm to wipe her face, she was surprised how wet her cheeks were. 'It just struck me how much I've missed home and now my only family isn't here any more.' Never would be again.

His hands were surprisingly gentle given how well he kept his emotions locked down. 'You have your daughter.'

Looking up at him, she nodded. 'True. I do. But now I'm the adult.'

His smile was the most genuine he'd given her. 'You'll manage. Very well, I think.'

The smile stabbed at her vulnerability. Etienne was the last person she should be exposing her emotions to, and yet she hadn't given it a thought, hadn't been aware how much she had shown him her true self. 'You're right, I will do better than manage. Elyna comes first.'

Etienne's head jerked up. 'Elyna?' He studied her once again with that intense look he did so well.

'Etienne, I need to tell you something.' She could barely hear herself speak over the thumping in her chest. She hadn't meant to say Elyna's name, but now it was out there the moment she'd been equally dreading and wanting was here.

'I'll be waiting in the car,' Alain said from somewhere behind them and moments later the door closed with a soft click.

'Elyna. My grandmother's name.' Etienne stared at her, disappointment filling his eyes, his face. Because he believed she'd used the name to try and manipulate him?

'Yes.'

The air whooshed out of Etienne's mouth. He stared at this apparition who was changing his world as she spoke. His heart pounded. How dared she? 'You've called her by my grandmother's name,' he snapped, fury whipping through him so fast he nearly lost his balance. Those strange feelings of intrigue and softness when he'd first laid eyes on the little girl now had an explanation—if he believed what Camille was hinting at. Did he? Not likely. How could he when his ex-fiancée had already tried to win him over with the same dubious methods? But this was Camille, the one woman he'd thought was better than that.

'Yes.'

'Why?' he snapped. She was using the child to get to him. What made him think she was different from any other woman who'd tried to trick him into a relationship? Camille was smarter, that was all. She'd gone deeper with her selfishness. Stupid, stupid, stupid man. He took a long breath in an attempt to calm down. Losing his temper would work in her favour, not his.

Camille leant down to place her daughter—not his—on the carpet. 'I think you've worked it out already.' Her mouth was grim, her blue eyes dark as storm clouds as she dropped the final bomb. 'Elyna is your daughter,' she said quietly, but firmly. No doubting she meant it.

Did that mean he had to accept this without question? No damned way. 'I'm supposed to believe you? Just like that?' What about that sense he'd had of being her father? It had to be wrong.

'You've got to be crazy to think I'll accept this based on your word.'

Camille's shoulders drooped. 'I never thought you would. You have issues around believing women when you think they might want something from you.'

'Low blow.' But true, he conceded to himself. 'So you used my grandmother's name to get to me?' Feeling blindsided again, he looked around and found himself gazing down at the little girl who sat on the floor staring up at him with those wide eyes. She was gorgeous. But his? Born eight weeks premature and eleven months old meant she could have been conceived eighteen months ago during their fling, if they'd been exclusive, which he suspected they were. Camille wasn't like that. Another sucker punch. His head whirled. This was insane.

'I would never do that.' Camille sank down onto a chair, her arms tight around her body. At least the tears had stopped, making it easier to watch her without softening towards her. 'While I was pregnant I believed I was having a boy. When I had a scan I didn't even ask for verification. I had a name picked out, and bought blue clothes. When the baby was born I was stunned. I know it sounds stupid, but it's how I felt. I had to choose another name and went with your grandmother's. I found it online.'

He started to speak but Camille talked right over him.

'Give me a moment to explain. I love the name Elyna. But I also wanted her to have some connection with your f-family.' She spluttered to a stop.

His heart heaved. If Camille was telling the truth, then he was indeed a father. Father to that lovely little girl watching him, her face filled with innocence, as if begging him to accept her. Strange how his usual reaction to a woman trying to pull a trick on him wasn't rushing to the fore as heavily as usual. Did he actually believe Camille? Or did he simply want to and just didn't know where to go from here? Not likely.

'Were you ever going to tell me? If we hadn't bumped into each other at the airport, would you have come to see me?'

'That was my first priority on returning home.'

'Oh, really?' Sarcasm dripped off his tongue. He wasn't doing very well, being snippy, but this was frightening. Being told by a woman she was carrying his child when she hadn't been was bad enough, but he'd held Elyna in his arms, which made things so much harder to push aside. He drew a breath to apologise for his rudeness but Camille cut him off.

'Really. Etienne...' She paused, seemed to gather strength from deep inside. Locking worried eyes on him, she continued. 'Do you remember that time I turned up at your office when you were on the phone talking to your mother?' She didn't wait for an answer. 'I'd come to tell you then.'

He remembered as clearly as if it had been yesterday because he'd often wondered if Camille had overheard him being so cynical. He'd been ashamed that she might've. 'You overheard me saying that no one had played the pregnancy card on me for a while.' That wasn't an excuse though. If, and it was still a big if, he was Elyna's father she still owed it to him to have told him.

'Would you have believed me? Be honest, Etienne.'

She had him there. He wouldn't have. Instead he'd have dragged up every reason not to after Melina trying the same trick.

Camille nodded. 'Exactly. Believe me, I wanted you to know. Yet I walked away without a word because you obviously wouldn't have accepted the truth. That's when I decided to go it alone and never tell you.'

'You just said it was a priority to tell me.' Nothing added up, which was too much like how conversations with Melina had generally gone.

'It is.' Her hands were clenched together so tight they were white. 'I was wrong to think I'd never tell you. When we were in Montreal, my grandmother pointed out you deserved to know. What you do about it is another issue.' She shivered. 'Elyna also deserves to know you're her father. Growing up, I didn't know mine and it was hard. I don't want that for Elyna.'

He wasn't getting sidetracked by that. 'So you believe you were wrong not to tell me before she was born?'

Camille straightened her back and locked a formidable look on him. 'I do but nothing I say can change what's happened. I am truly sorry but I was only protecting myself and Elyna.'

'You think that little of me?' That was new.

'Remember what I overheard? You were expecting another woman to try to fool you about a pregnancy. That made me realise you trusted no one. I wasn't going to listen to you tell me as much. I'm not perfect by any means but I am honest, especially when it's important.'

If words could burn he'd be seared. 'And me knowing about Elyna's important now?'

'Yes. For all of us.'

'You left the hospital on leave, but you could've come to see me there later on, or phoned me to arrange a meeting.'

She straightened her back further and lifted her chin, but her hands were shaking. 'I left for Canada two days later. Grandma was taking my grandfather's ashes over to be buried in his family plot and I went with her as she'd been there for me my whole life. I'd never have let her go on her own even when she had Grandpa's brothers to stay with. She was frail and unwell, but we meant to return home within three months and once I decided to tell you I fully intended seeing you before Elyna was born. Except Grandma became very ill with heart failure and couldn't fly home. I stayed out there with her until the end.'

Despite all the emotions filling him, the strongest was sorrow for Camille. Her obvious pain at her loss was unavoidable. 'Hell, Camille.' No wonder she'd broken down in tears when she walked in here. It took all his self-control not to go and haul her into his arms and hold her tight.

Damn it, he was letting her win him over already. What was wrong with him? He never trusted women when it came to getting close. He and Camille weren't that close, or even heading that way, but her putting it into words that he was Elyna's father had floored him. He might actually want it to be true, but it wasn't easy to let go of the past and move on. Time to get back to the red flag hanging between them.

'There are phones in Canada.' Sarcasm was the lowest form of wit, but right now his head was all over the place and he didn't know where he was going with this other than listening to the deep-seated need to protect himself. The fact he hadn't walked out already was another warning sign. He might believe Camille and that was so outrageous he couldn't breathe properly.

Camille winced. 'I deleted your number when

our fling finished. When I tried to get it from your secretary at the hospital, she refused to give it to me, and on my third attempt she made some very rude comments and hung up.'

'I left Paris to do a nine-month contract in Nice about two months after you went away.'

'So your secretary lied to me when she said you'd told her to tell me to get lost.'

'She did.' He had no idea what that was about.

Elyna gave a frustrated cry.

Camille scooped her up in her arms. 'Sorry, sweetheart. I promised you warm food and then forgot.' She kissed her girl's forehead. 'Come on. Let's see what Liza's put in the fridge for you.'

Again Etienne felt his heart do some crazy thumps. Camille and Elyna together made a lovely, heart-wrenching picture. But he couldn't just accept he had a role in this little family's lives without going through all the questions threatening to stymy him. Could he? No damned way. Melina had told him she was carrying his child when she hadn't even been pregnant. What was to say Camille wasn't using another trick to get him to fall into her trap?

Watching her holding Elyna while removing a container of food from the fridge he saw nothing to say she was lying to him. She was comfortable with Elyna, and didn't keep peeking at him to see how he was reacting. She wasn't nagging him to accept her news. Instead she was giving him space. Unheard of in his experience. There came the cynic again. Time to put it away? Could be. He crossed to the kitchen area and took the plastic container out of Camille's hand. 'Let me do that.'

She stepped out of his way, looking a little shocked. 'Are you sure?'

'Right now I'm not sure about anything, but I can do this while you comfort your daughter.' *My daughter, too?*

Elyna was still unsettled and her tiny fists were punching the air between her and her mother's breasts.

'Only warm it to a point you can still dip your finger in without it getting too hot.' Camille was watching him as he found a dish and spoon, wariness filling her face.

He liked that she was prepared to tell him what to do despite what hung between them. 'I've done this for my nephews.'

She shrugged as if to say, So what? 'I get a bit paranoid when it comes to Elyna.'

'Fair enough.' He had no doubts about her being a fiercely protective mother. He'd seen her looking out for patients when something went wrong and that came nowhere near what she'd do for her child. 'Who's Liza?' It wasn't important but he needed a moment or ten to catch up with everything. Not that it was working. He couldn't get past the fact Camille had confessed he was

Elyna's father. Despite his earlier suspicions it was as if the ground had been taken out from beneath him and he were standing on air. He was a father. Truly? He focused on preparing to heat the mushy food. Easier than working out where his emotions were with this.

Camille's mouth was tight. 'Liza's my best friend. We shared an apartment in our twenties. She's Elyna's surrogate aunt and would have her if anything happens to me.'

His stomach plummeted. If he was the father then that was something he should've had a say in, like the little girl's name, though he couldn't argue with the one Camille had chosen—other than he had initially thought it had been used as another way of sucking him in. Go carefully, he warned himself. It still could be. 'Why did you think you needed someone to step up to that role?'

'I don't have any family to be there for Elyna if something happens to me.'

'If what you say is true then she'd have me, and my extended family,' he snapped. This hurt. Badly. Because he *was* already accepting Camille mightn't be lying about his role in this little girl's life. Father. Parent. He swore under his breath. This was the last thing he'd expected when he'd boarded the plane in New York many hours ago. But why would it have occurred to him he had a child? Camille hadn't rushed to tell him about her pregnancy or make demands of him. *She came to see me at the hospital before she went away.*

'I did mess up, I admit that, but I deserved better, to be a part of the pregnancy, and the birth if possible, especially since she came so early,' he said quietly.

'So you do believe she's your daughter?' Was that hope in her face?

'It's too soon to say. There's a lot I still don't know.' He drew a steadying breath. If he wasn't truthful, how could he get annoyed if Camille wasn't? Except so far she appeared to be only honest. 'What you overheard that night didn't encourage you to talk to me but you didn't try again.'

'You'd have changed your mind about my pregnancy just like that?'

She had him there. It was seeing Elyna in the flesh that snagged at him and brought questions about her parentage to the fore. 'That's not the point. You should've tried,' he repeated stubbornly.

'I'd been dreading telling you since you always made it clear relationships weren't for you. I wasn't looking for one either, but once I heard you say something about not ever wanting children, I couldn't stay.' She certainly didn't hold back.

He drew a shaky breath. 'Fine. I'm prepared to hear what you have to say and go from there.'

Camille slumped against the bench. Again

tears filled those eyes that had unexpectedly followed him into sleep some nights when he'd been feeling lonely for company with a woman who'd want him for himself and not the family fortunes. That was definitely something he was not mentioning to her. Not now and maybe never. She slapped her hand across her eyes to clear away the moisture. 'Etienne, I am truly sorry.'

Once more she'd taken the wind out of him. It wasn't her words. No, all too often he'd heard those before. But never had he so keenly felt the sorrow, believed the genuine feeling behind the apology.

'I should've stayed that night and told you the truth, but it wasn't easy after hearing what you said. It hadn't been easy before that. Nor was it any easier when Elyna arrived.'

'I shouldn't have said what I did to my mother.' If he wasn't back-pedalling then what was he doing?

'You weren't to know what I'd come to tell you. You weren't even aware I was there.'

'True.' But he realised he would've reacted exactly as she'd expected if he'd known. He really had become a less than decent man over the years. Melina had stolen his trust, but he couldn't blame her for how he'd regarded other women. There were plenty who'd done all they could to win him over, but there had to be many more decent women if he'd only stopped to take a long hard look.

The microwave pinged. Relieved to have something mundane to do, he opened the door and removed the bowl to stir the mush. Mundane? If Elyna really was his daughter then there was nothing humdrum about preparing her food. Was she his? 'She doesn't look anything like me.' Or her relatives on his side. Ouch. Was that acceptance of the fact she was his? No. Too soon to be certain. But then how to go about finding out? A DNA test would give him the answer he needed but he wasn't keen. Too clinical. He wanted to know more about everything else, like what Camille expected from him regarding shared parenting and where she'd live. His head was telling him one thing and his heart another, and until they were on the same page nothing would be clear.

Was Camille like everyone else and just trying to get what she wanted from him? Or was she honest when she said she was looking out for her daughter? How was he supposed to know the answer to that or all the other frightening doubts roiling in his brain? Creating doubts that suggested he might be looking at Camille differently from how he normally approached women. Face it, he liked her a lot. Enough to have tried to find out where she'd gone after leaving her job at the hospital. He hadn't got far, wary of being seen to be too interested in her. No one he'd asked at the hospital had known where she'd gone, other than her being on extended leave, and when he'd gone around to her old apartment, he'd been told she no longer lived there.

Camille reached for the bowl, dipped her finger into the pumpkin-coloured mush. 'Perfect.'

He presumed she was referring to Elyna's meal. 'We have a long way to go yet.'

'Absolutely.' Camille settled Elyna into the high chair Liza had provided, still amazed that Etienne hadn't left by now. He'd been shocked, even snippy at times, but altogether he was a lot calmer than she'd expected. 'I'm ready to talk about anything when it comes to Elyna, whenever you want.'

'I appreciate that. So Elyna's Canadian?'

Going for formal now? It could've been worse, though it did make her feel oddly out of place. 'With Elyna being born in Canada I applied for her French citizenship.'

'So she has dual citizenship?'

'Yes.' Was that so bad? 'I intend raising her here so it made sense to do that straight away.'

He was still staring at her, but she could see her words sinking in. 'I understand what you're saying, Camille. I wouldn't have expected any less of you. It just occurred to me that she was Canadian by birth, that's all.'

So he was more shocked than he'd shown. 'Thank you.' Those darned tears were back. She rubbed her face. 'You must be wishing you hadn't seen me at the airport.'

He gave a tight smile. 'It's been an interesting couple of hours I hadn't predicted.' Then he asked, 'Can I make you coffee? Or get you something else to drink?'

He'd do that for her when he was still so rattled by her news? He wasn't an unkind man but he had surprised her as she'd thought he'd want to keep aloof while they got down to business. Yet somehow he'd understood her distress, which was more than she did right now. She was all over the place with her feelings about Etienne, Elyna, coming home, everything. The tension holding her tight backed off a notch. 'Coffee would be lovely, thanks.'

'Mind if I have one too?'

'Of course not.' She was hardly going to say no when he was being polite. *Relax, Etienne. It's been a shock, yes, but I'm not going to spring any demands on you. Unless you decide you want to take my daughter away from me, that is, and then you'll have a battle like none you've ever known.*

'I think a certain little girl wants to go down.' There was a glint of amusement in his grey eyes. Eyes she'd never forgotten since she'd left his bed for the last time.

Elyna had gobbled down her food and was

now trying to push out of the high chair. Thankfully the strap prevented her winning that battle. 'Come on, little one. Let's set you free to rush around and use up some of that energy fizzing through you.'

On the floor Elyna headed off, crawling to the chairs and then the coffee table. Looking at her phone, Camille gasped. 'Where's the time gone?' Hours had passed since the plane had landed.

'Time flies when you're having fun,' Etienne quipped, surprising her yet again.

Fun? Right. Though it was a relief he wasn't sticking to the hard-nosed man whose life had just been tipped upside down, she conceded. 'Do you really want coffee? Or would you prefer wine?' It might help lighten the mood between them and she'd seen a bottle of Chenin Blanc in the fridge, thanks to Liza.

Etienne stepped back from the coffee machine. 'You've got me.' He removed his phone from his jacket pocket. 'I'll tell Alain to go home. I'll grab a taxi home later.'

Damn. She'd walked into that one. Coffee would've been drunk quicker and he might've been on his way sooner. Not a lot she could say though. Looking around, she spied her girl trying to climb up one of the bookcases and rushed across. 'No, Elyna, get off there.' If the bookcase tipped she'd get hurt with a lot of bruises to colour her pale skin. Snatching her daughter up in her arms, she kissed both cheeks and took her over to the sofa to put her down. 'I see I'm going to have to keep a sharp eye on you.'

'You need to get someone to put some screws through the back of the bookcase to fix it to the wall if she's going to become a little monkey.' Etienne was gazing at Elyna as he poured wine into the glasses he'd found. There was a look of need in his eyes, as though he really wanted Elyna to be his daughter.

He was as vulnerable as she was, Camille realised with a shock. Throughout their fling she'd only known him to wear a kind yet aloof face. Even more so at work with his patients and their families. The staff were also kept at bay with that look. Everyone thought the world of Dr Etienne Laval, but no one ever got behind his barriers. Not even her when they were between the sheets, naked as the day they were born, being physically intimate and yet mentally separate. 'I'll get onto it tomorrow, find a handyman online.'

Etienne said tightly, 'I'll do it after I finish work one evening this coming week.' He seemed to be taking over already.

Not likely. 'That won't be necessary. I'll be here all day. I resigned when I was in Montreal longer than expected, and I still haven't got a new job yet. The two interviews I've set up are three days away.'

'I said I'd do it, Camille. Why are you looking for work when you've got Elyna to take care of?'

She turned to stare at him. *Here we go, getting to the crux of his deep concerns over being used.* Fair enough. He had every right to find out as much as possible about how she was raising their daughter, and what she didn't expect from him. 'I need to work, though not full-time. Liza runs a crèche nearby.' At Central Hospital. 'Elyna will go to her when I can't be here.' *Don't try and argue with me.* 'We've got it sorted.'

'I expect to partake in decisions about Elyna's life if I accept she's mine.'

Did that mean he *was* accepting her as his daughter? Or was he looking for other ways she might be trying to get something from him? 'We will talk about everything and I'm happy to work things out together, but I wasn't here when I applied for the positions, and I had to get things organised for Elyna as soon as possible.'

'Where have you applied for positions?'

She named the hospitals. 'I've talked online to the head nurses at both places and now need to meet up and take a look around.'

'You don't sound overly enthusiastic about either of them.'

He was too observant. She shouldn't be surprised. He'd always been so. 'You're right. But it's hard to suss out things online. I like to get the feel of where I might work before making up my mind.' If only she could go back to the surgical ward at Central Hospital. She'd considered ringing the head nurse, Karina, to see if there might be a position open but that would mean working alongside Etienne, which wasn't a good idea until they'd sorted out where they were going with Elyna, and then only if it was going well between them. That was if he'd even returned there after working in Nice. 'Where are you working now?'

Etienne didn't answer, instead asking her a question. 'What about your old job?' He was watching her closely as he handed over a glass. 'I don't doubt you'd be taken on in a flash if there's a position available.'

He was putting that out there despite the bomb she'd dropped on him? Because he was accepting of her or wanted to keep a close eye on everything she did regarding Elyna? Locking eyes with him, she said, 'Do you think that's wise? I mean, we have a lot to sort out and, if you're still at Central, working side by side might crank up the tension, not defuse it.'

'I do still work there and I get where you're coming from, but I reckon we're both better than that. We worked well together during and after our fling. Sure, this is deeper and there're a lot more issues to get through, but I believe neither of us would make it difficult at work.'

She was completely perplexed as to where she

stood. Etienne was being genuinely positive about Elyna so she needed to reciprocate for all their sakes. She'd also far prefer to take a position at Central than anywhere else. It'd been the best job ever and though she couldn't expect to walk back into the same role it would be fabulous working in a familiar environment when she had so much else to deal with. 'I'll think about it.'

He flicked her a small smile. 'Good. Do you still have the same phone number?'

He hadn't wiped her number when they'd finished? She nodded. 'I have. This is weird.'

Etienne sat down at the table opposite her, wine in hand. 'You're absolutely certain I'm Elyna's father, aren't you?'

What? The man could change subjects faster than a blink. 'Yes.'

No comment came her way.

She tried again. 'Look, I know you're going to have lots of questions about Elyna and I have no problem answering them.'

'You bet I do.'

Despite her knowing that'd been coming, his abrupt reply still hurt. 'I did not sleep with anyone else prior to or during our fling.' There hadn't been anyone since either but that wasn't something he needed to know as it did not affect his paternity. She didn't want him feeling sorry for her because she hadn't had anyone else in her life recently. He wouldn't know how wary of getting involved with men she was, and that even a short fling like theirs had been rare for her. He'd no doubt have had his share of women since she'd walked away from him. She hadn't known she was pregnant at the time. That news had come later, knocking her to her knees, and making working with him those last days difficult. If only she'd told him the night she'd gone to his office then this would all be over and the decisions made—or they'd currently be doing battle in the courts.

Etienne sipped his wine while he studied her, a raft of emotions flitting across his face, the strongest of which appeared to be embarrassment and that was something she'd never expected.

When the silence went on too long she couldn't take it any more. 'Any comment?'

His eyes darkened to a deep steely grey. 'I'm sorry you heard what I said to my mother.'

'Even if I'd still had your number I wanted to tell you face to face so you could see I was being truthful. I also wanted to see your initial reactions.'

'I think I understand that.'

What? Etienne wasn't trying to make her feel bad? Long-held caution kept her wary. She did not accept he wouldn't have more to say. No doubt he needed time to think about everything so it was possible he was waiting for another day to lay out his true feelings about what she'd done, then follow up with what the cost to her heart was going to be in terms of Elyna. 'Everything changed when Grandma became so ill. She was my priority after caring for Elyna.' The guilt over letting down Etienne rose once more, threatening to choke her. This wasn't getting any easier.

The sound of little knees and hands slapping the carpet coming towards him made Etienne smile despite the turmoil going on in his head. So he had a daughter. That was if he could believe Camille when she said he was the father. For one, she hadn't rushed to let him know with a list of demands in her hand. Secondly, he really couldn't find it in him to believe she'd lie to him. That was foolish because enough other women had worked hard at trying to convince him of one falsehood or another, but if in doubt, he only had to think about how Camille had been the one to call off their fling, not him, to realise she was different. *If* he was truly honest, he'd been disappointed when she had. They'd got on so well, and there hadn't been any problems with their relationship. It was a fling and Camille accepted that, hadn't looked for anything else.

Yet when she'd left he'd realised he'd been coming to want more from her. Which had scared the pants off him and made him determined to protect himself. But it had backfired. Instead he had become restless, especially after Camille had quit nursing on the ward where he'd worked. So restless that he'd taken up the nine-month contract in Nice that his friend, Fillip, had offered him.

Yet the restlessness had continued and he'd begun to feel a little lonely, as though he was missing out on something important. Spending time with Fillip and his wife, Torrie, and their kids didn't help, only made him finally see what he was missing out on and accept the deep-seated need to have a family of his own that he'd been denying himself. But letting go the restraints he'd placed around his heart didn't come easy. Now it appeared he might have to—if he truly believed Elyna was his.

'Up.' Elyna was staring at Etienne. 'Up.'

'Persistent, aren't you?' Persistent and cute. Even knowing lifting Elyna into his arms was going to undermine his determination to keep her at a distance until he was absolutely certain he was her father, Etienne couldn't resist.

'Very,' Camille agreed. 'Apparently it's normal.'

Turning away from Camille's all-seeing eyes, he drew a ragged breath. She was the last person he wanted to notice his vulnerability. This had turned into one hell of a day, one of the worst he'd known in a long time. And maybe one of the best, too.

After a drawn-out moment that chilled him he turned back. 'Camille...' He paused. Was he about to go too far, to make her believe he was an easy target? Or was he actually moving forward, accepting her for who she really was? Would it be wonderful if he could do that?

'Yes, Etienne?'

'This isn't easy for either of us. I am trying to work my way through it all because it's so important,' he added, and immediately hoped he'd never regret saying that.

'Thank you.'

He got his smile. It hit him hard in the solar plexus. She was beautiful—add in that smile and there were no words to describe her. Other than beautiful, and caring, and just what he wanted in his for-ever woman if he could finally let go of the shackles holding him back.

'Would you like another glass of wine before you head away?' she suddenly asked.

He should call a taxi, get home and have that shower he'd been promising himself from the moment he'd walked off the plane, but he couldn't find it in him to turn Camille down. He needed more time with her. He wasn't entirely certain why but he truly did want to be with Camille at the moment. Scary maybe, but for once he couldn't find it in himself to haul up the usual barriers and act like the arrogant man he was often called. He did behave arrogantly at times to hide the despair he felt at not being able to trust a woman and therefore most likely never going to have his happy ever-after that, until Melina had lied about her pregnancy, he'd always believed was a natural part of adulthood.

'Yes, I'd like that.' Sitting drinking wine with a woman he wasn't close to was rare, and made him feel light-headed in a strangely happy kind of way. No matter what Camille had done regarding Elyna, and the jury was slowly coming round to her side, he wanted to unwind from a massive day. Long-haul flights were always tiring, but this exhaustion was all to do with the other problems thrown at him in the last few hours. 'Would there be a red available?'

'Do you like Merlot?'

He nodded, exhaustion taking over. Which was why he should leave. 'Definitely.'

'Then it's your lucky day. Liza left a bottle in the cupboard.' Camille grimaced. 'Sorry, I meant—'

He held his hand up. 'It's fine. I know what you meant.'

Her smile returned, and he found himself relaxing some more. So easy to do, which was odd when he'd usually be thinking of the reason behind every single word she uttered, every one of those smiles she gave him, every move she made. Seemed that the cynic was taking a back seat for once. He knew it wouldn't remain there, but it felt good, almost exhilarating, to be free of his other persona for a while.

'Good,' Camille said as she got out fresh glasses.

Elyna tapped his chin with her tiny fist. She was such a cutey. His heart did a flip. This was really his daughter? Who'd have believed he was a father? Certainly not him. Did that mean he did now? he wondered yet again. He wasn't quite one hundred per cent there yet, but yes, he could admit to himself he was well on the way. Elyna was already moving into his heart, making him soften towards her as she stared up at him with her mother's stunning eyes.

'Hello, little one. You've got food all over your face.' Looking over to the kitchen, he saw a cloth on the counter. 'I'll wipe it clean.' He made to stand up, but didn't really want to lose that soft touch where her hand lay.

'Here, use this.' Camille was already there, curiosity filling her face.

Of course she was on edge about his reactions and what he thought, and this was another step, although she wouldn't know in which direction. *Join the club, Camille.* 'Hey, Elyna, let me wipe away that sticky stuff for you.'

Elyna tipped her head sideways, eyes shut tight, as was her mouth.

Laughter bubbled up through his chest. 'She's not afraid of me one little bit.'

'Why should she be? You're not a monster.' Camille returned to pouring the wine. 'I have tried to warn her about those, though she hasn't a clue what I'm talking about.'

'She's very young for that, surely?' The goo came off Elyna's face and she opened her eyes again. Snatching the cloth, she held it to her chest as though she'd won a prize as she wriggled down to the floor again.

'Like I said, I'm ultra cautious when it comes to my girl.' She handed him a glass.

'Thanks.' Raising it in a salute: 'To sorting this out without too many difficulties.'

She nodded and took a sip of her wine before saying, 'I'd prefer none of those but that's being naïve.'

'Naïve is the last thing you are.' The Merlot was good. Not one from his family's estate but nearly as good. He was biased but that was what good families were all about. Leaning back in the seat, he closed his eyes for a long moment. Easier than looking at Camille and remembering the fantastic body her clothes covered. Safer than remembering kissing his way from her mouth down to her core, or recalling sliding inside her to be surrounded by glorious heat.

Enough. He sat up in a hurry and red wine sloshed over his trousers. Clamping his mouth shut over the oath that sprang to his tongue, he glared at Camille as though she was at fault. Of course she was. If he hadn't been thinking about her the wine would still be in the glass.

'You'd better take those pants off so I can run cold water over the wine.'

Take my trousers off? Here, in front of you? No, thanks. There'd be no stopping him reacting to her in a completely wrong way. 'I'll be fine. I'd better get a move on.' He was suddenly in a hurry to get away and put some space between them so he could think more clearly. Standing up, he said, 'I'll be in touch.'

'What's your number?' Stress darkened her eyes as she nibbled her bottom lip. Far more worried than she'd let on?

He couldn't stop looking at her. His heart was pounding with similar worry. He wanted to hold her and say everything would be all right. But first he had to believe it himself. 'I'll send you a text so you have it.' His feet didn't move. Instead his arms lifted of their own volition and he placed his hands on her shoulders. She was shaking. 'Camille.' What could he say to make everything better? His hands tightened as her warmth stole into his palms. Leaning nearer, he drank in the sight of her lips, recalled the feeling of them on his skin, teasing him, tormenting him. An overwhelming need to kiss her tore through him.

Camille stared at him, her mouth slightly open as though waiting for his kiss.

Torment. This was ridiculous. She'd dealt him a body blow like no other. There were huge problems hovering between them and he wanted to kiss her? That would be the worst thing he could do. Spinning around, he strode out of the apartment without a backward glance. Camille was not getting to him. Not at all.

Tell that to someone who'd believe him.

CHAPTER THREE

'WHO'S RINGING AT this hour?' Camille groaned as she rolled over in bed two mornings later, still worn out from the flight home and how her mind never stopped thinking about Etienne and what he intended to do about Elyna.

Nine-thirty.

What? It couldn't be. Elyna would've woken her by now demanding food and cuddles.

The phone was still playing her favourite tune. She didn't recognise the number. 'Hello, Camille Beauregard speaking.'

'Camille, this is Karina Prout. Welcome home. How are you? You've been gone for ever.'

What was this about? She hadn't applied for a position back at Central Hospital. 'Hello, Karina. I'm good, glad to be home at last.'

'I heard you're looking for a job and want you back here. We've missed you.'

She hadn't expected that. Seemed Etienne had talked to Karina so he obviously still had no qualms about working together. 'Did Etienne mention I can't work a full week, that I require part-time hours?'

'Yes, he did.'

Did she want to work on his ward? It'd be all right when things were going well, but what about the days when they might be at a stand-off?

'He also told me why. Congratulations on becoming a mum. It's awesome news.'

She didn't know the half of it. 'I don't know, Karina. I loved working there but things have changed.'

'Come and have a chat. No pressure,' Karina laughed.

She had nothing to lose. 'All right. I'll be there today at one if that suits you.' Liza's crèche was at the hospital so leaving Elyna there for a little while shouldn't be a problem. If only Liza were here. But she had amazing staff covering for her while she was in Marseilles.

'Something for you to think about is do you want to do five half-day shifts per week or three full days? We can accommodate you either way since you've got a wee child to consider.'

It sounded as if she already had the job. There was a shortage of nurses at the moment, but this was happening fast. 'I think I'd prefer five half-days. That way Elyna isn't at a crèche all day.' And she'd get fun time with her every day.

'Sounds good to me. I wouldn't have wanted my daughter spending long days in a childcare facility at that age either. You've got the half-days.' Karina laughed again. 'That sounds like I've sent your name forward to have you signed on already, but I'm sure you know where I'm coming from.'

Camille found herself laughing too. It felt good to hear Karina agree with her choice. Solo parenting meant every decision was up to her, and sometimes she liked to know she was on the right track, even over something like work hours. 'I'm looking forward to catching up with you.'

'Hopefully the job's what you're looking for. Oh, got to go. See you later.' Click. The phone went silent.

Camille stared at it. Had that really happened or was she dreaming? No, that was Karina. Etienne must have told the head nurse she was looking for work. So he intended keeping her close, for whatever reason, adding to her confusion and wariness. She leapt off the bed and grabbed her robe. Because she'd thought he worked there all the time she was away she'd never checked to see if there was a position available. They did work well together, but that had been before Elyna.

Would they be able to get along just as well when it came to raising Elyna? She had her own ideas on being a parent and the last thing she wanted was Etienne taking over completely. Would he though? She had no idea. He hadn't contacted her since he left on Sunday night, which surprised her. Guess he'd been assimilating everything and making some decisions about what he was going to do about it. All she could do was wait to hear from him and deal with each problem as it arose. She'd been relieved to have some time to get used to the fact he now knew about Elyna. She no longer had to face that worry, but there were a lot more things hanging in the air regarding what happened next. Waiting to talk about everything wasn't her style now the main issue was out there, but she knew she had to give him time or everything would explode faster than a hand grenade.

Suddenly rare excitement tripped through Camille. She really was back home. She still couldn't believe she'd slept in after finally falling asleep well after midnight. She hadn't the night before, worrying about his reaction to her news. Like on Sunday night when she'd first gone to bed he'd been on her mind, first as a problem over their daughter, but then it was the memory of his long, well-built body wrapped around her as he made love to her so tenderly taking over her thoughts until she finally fell asleep. Now he was back, foremost in her mind again.

'Mama. Mama, up.'

Swinging around, she lifted Elyna from the cot and into her arms. 'Hello, my girl, you've had a big sleep.' Not a peep all night. Showed how tired she'd been too. Bringing the cot into her bedroom might've helped. She hadn't wanted Elyna waking and thinking she was in a strange place and Mummy not there. She'd leave it in here for a couple more days before putting it in the bedroom that had been hers growing up. 'Oh, Grandma, Grandpa, I miss you both so much,' she sniffed.

'Down.' Wriggle, wriggle.

Back to reality. Icky nappies and grumpy child. 'Let's change your nappy first.'

'No.'

After a few minutes' debate Camille finally had the nappy changed and Elyna's face washed and now her daughter was charging around the apartment on her hands and knees as if she was on an adventure, happy not to be constrained.

Her favourite tune played again. This time, Etienne's name lit up the screen.

She wasn't ready to talk to him. He might spoil her good mood, but avoidance wasn't her style. Except when she'd overheard how he was waiting to be lied to about a pregnancy. 'Morning.'

'Morning, Camille. Thought I'd better warn you I told Karina you were back and looking for work.'

Shouldn't he be operating at this time of the day? He always used to have a heavy schedule and nothing should've changed in the time she'd been away. He was nothing if not predictable about his work routine. He said it made for easier days and less stress for patients. 'Too late. She's already called and I'm going in to see her today.

She's given me a choice of which hours like she's already arranged the contract.'

'Good. Anyway, I'm between ops so talk later.'

Was that a promise? She started to reply then realised he'd gone. Great. He'd just pricked her happy bubble by reminding her that he had no problem with coming and going in her life as he saw fit. Time for a shower, food and getting outside for a walk in the park, she decided.

'Ready,' the anaesthetist told Etienne. 'Obs are good.'

Picking up the scalpel, Etienne shoved everything else out of his mind. His patient did not need him reflecting on Camille and how she affected him just by being herself. 'This should be straightforward but the growth is large so complications could arise,' he told the team at the operating table. Colleen Willows had a massive lump on her colon, which appeared cancerous on the X-ray.

'That's a biggie,' the junior doctor commented a while later when Etienne removed the fibroid.

One of the nurses shuddered. 'Why didn't she notice something wasn't right? It's not like she wouldn't have had some indicators, surely?'

Behind his mask, Etienne grimaced. 'Her husband said that, despite a family history of bowel cancer, she ignored his pleas to see her doctor. It's like she's been in denial.' Which he'd never understand. He'd dealt with similar situations before, and knew there was no understanding some people, but that didn't make it any easier for him to deal with the situation. There were downsides to being a doctor.

'It still doesn't make any sense,' the nurse muttered.

'I agree.' Etienne concentrated on tying off blood vessels before suturing the incisions he'd made earlier. The growth he'd removed had been placed in sterile bags to be sent to the laboratory to be studied under a microscope. The X-ray showed signs of the disease but only when a pathologist examined the sample could it be signed off as positive or negative. As with all his patients, he fervently hoped Colleen would come through the treatment that lay ahead in good shape.

A little over two hours after making the first incision into Colleen's abdomen, Etienne stepped back from the table and straightened his back. 'Done.' He'd check on her later in the day when she was settled into the surgical ward.

The ward where very possibly Camille would soon be nursing. Camille. The moment he didn't have a patient to focus on she slammed back into his mind. He'd never forgotten her after their fling. Hard to do when they'd continued to work alongside each other, but even when she'd left the ward he hadn't been able to put her in the past. Something about her seemed to like hanging around, keeping him aware of her in ways he hadn't experienced in a long time. Since Melina he'd become very self-protective in matters of the heart. Possibly too protective, but how else was he supposed to remain safe? Now that seemed to have blown up in his face with the arrival of Camille and her daughter back in town.

After she'd left the hospital she'd seemed to have cut contact with those she'd worked with. Hearing what she'd had to cope with in Montreal, he understood. He hadn't tried too hard to find her either, because that would have shown he was interested in what she was up to and it was bad enough admitting it to himself, let alone anyone else figuring it out. He was known to only have flings and nothing deeper. Not that most women took any notice, often persisting with the *'I'm the one'* thing he never fell for.

Except Camille. She hadn't hung around, hadn't asked anything more of him than some fun time together in bed. Of course she'd piqued his interest by being different, but not enough for him to think she could be special. Yet he had missed her. A lot more than he would've believed.

Now Camille was back and had told him he was the father of her daughter, and while his instincts were in denial, his heart was sending different messages that had him in a right state wondering what to do next. In the early stage of her pregnancy she hadn't hung around expecting to be financially supported and taken into his family as his wife. Instead she'd gone away to support her grandmother at a difficult time. Neither had she rushed to let him know he had a daughter once Elyna was born. She certainly hadn't made any demands on Sunday, either, although that had been a hectic and emotional day as it was. Learning he was supposedly Elyna's father had rocked him to his roots. Plus woken him up to all sorts of possibilities. Good ones—and not so wonderful ones.

As he scrubbed his hands he kept picturing Camille smiling at Elyna. She'd even smiled at him occasionally, though warily. She'd poured *him* a glass of wine when he was too exhausted to head away. After a long-haul flight with a toddler, coming across him at the airport and then telling him her child was also his, she must've been more shattered than he had, yet she'd been nothing but open and caring.

Ahh, not always open, he reminded himself. She hadn't discussed much about Elyna and what she expected of him if he accepted his role in her daughter's life. While he was accepting it far more quickly than he'd have believed possible, he wasn't quite ready to tell Camille yet. The barriers were still firmly in place when it came to protecting himself. He needed time to think about everything. For him the first question was, if he did step up, where would Camille and Elyna live?

Camille had a nice apartment in a good part of the city, but he wouldn't be moving in with her. It was too small. They'd be stepping around each other all the time. Anyway, he had a perfect house, which he had no intention of moving out of. Why would he when he had five bedrooms and bathrooms, two lounges, a modern kitchen and a gym? If anyone was moving it should be Camille.

How would she take to that idea? Something made him think she wasn't going to rush in gleefully and make the most of his comfort and wealth. Of course, he could be making a huge mistake and really she was cleverer than he'd thought in getting everything she wanted. Except he didn't quite believe it. Camille had a heart of gold when it came to looking out for others, and the same would be true for Elyna, only many times stronger. Her love for Elyna was fierce, and so obvious a blind man could see it. And he wasn't blind. Except in the love department.

His head spun. There was no way of knowing what was going to happen until he'd spent more time with Camille. Something he'd get on with sooner rather than later. In the meantime he'd go up to the ward to check two patients he'd operated on earlier.

As he stepped out of the elevator his senses

were immediately on high alert. A light laugh coming from the nurses' hub sent shivers of longing down his back. He'd know that gut-wrenching sound anywhere. Camille was here. Her interview should be over by now, surely? Did this mean she was keen to take the job before she'd even had the other interviews she'd lined up? He hoped so.

Not because he'd be able to keep an eye on her, but because she was one of the best nurses he'd worked with. Not to mention how much she intrigued him. She had him thinking outside the box when it came to his usual reactions to single women. Forget looking stunning and sexy, forget she was claiming he was the father of her daughter. What really rocked him was how she could look him in the eye and speak her mind without trying to be coy or cute or needy. Camille came across as real. Simple as that. Also as complex, because for him it was a rarity. His cynical side coming to the fore once again? Absolutely, but then that was what usually saved him from trouble. Was Camille trouble? Or a genuine woman who wanted nothing more than for him to be a good father to their daughter?

'Hey, Etienne, good news,' Karina called from the hub. 'Camille's agreed to come on board, starting next Monday.'

Camille turned to face him as he crossed to join them, surprise registering on her face. 'Etienne? What are you doing here?'

'I work here, remember?' he teased.

'You set me up.'

'I did.'

Camille stared at him for a moment longer before turning back to Karina, pure determination taking over. 'The job's perfect for where I'm at right now.' She looked back at him. 'I'm going to do five hours a day, five days a week.' *Don't even think about arguing with me*, said her steadfast gaze. 'I am not going to put Elyna in the crèche for full days. It'd be too much for her.'

Totally agreeing, he nodded once. 'Fair enough. Welcome back.'

For a brief instant Camille looked stunned. Hadn't she expected him to agree so readily when he'd told Karina she was back in town? The thing was, he agreed wholeheartedly with her decision. If she had to work, then shorter days were better for her too. 'Mornings or afternoons?'

'Both, depending on who else is working. Either way I'll be covering the middle of the day.'

So she'd be with his patients when they came up from Theatre. He found himself smiling far too easily. Whether for his patients or himself he wasn't sure, and he wasn't delving deeper to figure it out. Instead he'd enjoy the moment. 'Great.'

Camille's eyes widened briefly.

His smile grew. It was fun surprising her. 'I'm glad you've got this sorted.'

Karina cut through his thoughts. 'We're going

for a coffee unless there's something you need me for. We've got lots to discuss.'

'I'll leave you to it, then.' But his feet were glued to the floor as he watched Camille. 'How's Elyna? Got over her long day flying home?'

Camille appeared surprised he'd ask in front of Karina. 'She's all right, still a bit scratchy at times. Right now she's at Liza's crèche downstairs.'

The hospital crèche? Very convenient, and, yes, close to Camille's apartment. 'It was hard on her.' As it had been for him, though not because of the hours in the plane. Camille still looked tired around the edges too. Time to get back on track, and stop letting her distract him. 'Go and have that coffee, you two. There's nothing you need to hang around for regarding my patients, Karina. I presume the two women who came into the ward earlier are doing well?'

'They're both awake and comfortable. No problems.'

'Good to hear. I'll still check on them. There's another woman coming up shortly. I'll fill you in later.' He needed to stop talking and move away, but it wasn't easy. He liked being with Camille. Scary, right?

'Come on, Camille. Let's make the most of the quiet,' Karina said.

Camille watched her walk away before turning to him. 'Will I be seeing you this week?'

'Yes, tonight.'

Her eyebrows flew up. 'O-kay.'

Again he'd surprised her. Point to him. 'See you later.' He was being childish, but he wasn't used to dealing with a woman who could rattle him so easily. It might be good for him.

The emergency bell rang through the ward. Loud and demanding.

'Room five. I'll grab the gear.' Karina was already racing to get the emergency trolley.

Etienne nodded. 'I'm heading there.' He rushed down the corridor to room five.

Camille was right behind him, no doubt instincts of old kicking in. 'I'm here if needed.'

'Good.' Since she was about to start work here again there'd be no questions asked if she did get involved with helping the patient. 'Hopefully you're not required.'

Through the door of room five, he looked around, saw a man sprawled upside down half out of bed. 'Luca, what's happened?' He'd operated on him yesterday for liver cancer and he'd struggled with pain and mild after-effects of the anaesthetics. 'Luca?' Etienne reached the bed. 'Can you hear me?'

'I pressed the button,' a man in the next bed told him. 'He was lying back against his pillow like he was asleep but then the next thing he jerked about and slumped over the edge.'

Etienne had his hand around Luca's wrist trying to find a pulse. 'Nothing.'

Camille was at the other side of the bed, her fingers on the carotid artery. Unreal. The last time they'd worked on a patient together on this ward they'd dealt with a cardiac arrest. She shook her head. 'No pulse.'

With help from Camille on the opposite side pulling the man towards her, Etienne lifted Luca back onto the bed. 'Where's Karina with the trolley?' he demanded. There was a lot of phlegm dribbling from Luca's mouth. Had inflammation started in the liver where he'd operated?

'Right here. What do you need?' Karina said.

'Defibrillator.' The hospital gown covering Luca's upper body posed no problem as Etienne tore it down the front. He wasn't wasting a moment getting scissors from the trolley. This man was dying before their eyes. He immediately began compressions, not waiting for Karina to get the defib set up. This was *his* patient who'd come through a serious operation. He'd been reluctant to increase the analgesics any further as Luca was already on strong medications. At the time the heart indicators had been normal for post op with nothing to suggest there were any clots in his arteries, or inflammation around the wound site.

Camille was poised, ready to give Luca two breaths the moment he stopped the compressions.

Thank goodness for her. No other nurse had responded to the emergency.

'Where is everyone?' he asked on an intake of air.

'At lunch or seeing to patients coming up from Theatre,' Karina told him as she placed electrical pads on the exposed chest before them. 'We're short-staffed, remember?'

Another reason to be glad Camille was coming back to work here, he thought. No matter what lay between them, he was pleased about that. 'I repeat, welcome aboard, Camille. A bit sooner than you'd expected though.'

Her reply was a soft smile.

'Your turn,' he said with a return smile as he reached the thirtieth compression.

After giving Luca two breaths she stood back to let Karina finish setting up to send an electric current through him.

'Stand back, Etienne,' Karina warned before he could start more compressions.

He stepped away and watched Luca, digging deep for positivity that all would go well for his patient. It was entirely out of his hands now. All he could do was watch the green line running along the bottom of the defib screen and wait for it to lift up and down continuously.

It didn't.

Etienne clenched his hands together and began compressing down on Luca's heart once more while Karina got the defibrillator up to speed once more, all the while muttering, 'Come on, man. Don't let this happen. You can start breathing again. Now.'

The room was eerily quiet. No one else was talking, the other patients focused on what was going on.

'Stand back.'

He and Camille stepped away, watching the screen as the current struck.

Please, please, please, come back, Luca.

Luca's body jerked. The line lifted, dropped. Lifted again, and dropped, lifted once more, and then again and again.

In his chest, Etienne's heart thumped hard. 'Thank goodness for defibs and switched-on nurses.'

'And excellent doctors,' Camille said quietly beside him and squeezed his hand, this time surprising *him*.

She understood him so well. It brought a lump to his throat. He needed someone on his side right now. Not just anybody, but someone who knew him even a little. Camille.

Dressed in pyjamas, Elyna had been fed and bathed, and was charging around on her knees playing with her teddy bear. She squealed the ceiling down when the doorbell rang.

'This should be fun,' Camille said to herself. 'Parenting isn't all wine and roses.'

'Someone's excited,' Etienne commented with a small smile as he followed her into the apartment, and spotted the lively Elyna.

'I've tried putting her in my bed only to have her climb out and crawl out here, screaming as though I'd deprived her of everything she could possibly want. I'm surprised the neighbours haven't banged on the door to complain.' She doubted Mrs Auclair would do that, being a grandmother of three boisterous young boys, but sometimes when a person had had a bad day there was no accounting for what they'd say.

Elyna raced at Etienne and slammed into his legs, wrapping her little arms tight around his calves.

Etienne bent down to lift her up in his arms. 'Hello, Elyna. Did you tell Mummy I came to see you in the crèche today?'

Elyna stopped shrieking to stare at him, her eyes wide.

'You did? That's good, kiddo. Now, what's your problem? You can't still be overtired from your big day on the plane.'

Camille laughed. As if Elyna had a clue what he was saying, but he was being friendly and kind. Camille sighed. Why wouldn't he be? He wasn't an ogre. Unless he fought her for custody of their daughter. *Stop it. Give the man a chance to show where he's at first.* No doubt he'd still be coming to terms with her news and, despite indicating he might believe her on Sunday, with time to reflect he might've changed his mind. For now she'd accept how intrigued Elyna was with him and let everything else go. It seemed the only way to deal with the large pit in her stomach that had been growing bigger over the last hour as she'd waited for Etienne to turn up.

'I was told you'd dropped in.' She was taking it as an indicator he was beginning to accept the truth. 'I took Elyna to a park by the Seine on the way home and she went crazy crawling around with a little boy there with his mother. Once we got back here she crashed and slept on and off for the remainder of the afternoon, either in the pram or on the couch. I didn't put her to bed in the hope she'd fall asleep quickly after dinner. Seems I got that wrong.'

'From what my sister's said over the years she's been raising her little boys, there's no such thing as getting it right all the time when it comes to parenting.' Etienne was still looking at Elyna and his smile had grown.

Camille felt her heart skip a beat. Could this work out? He was a wonderful man when he wasn't wary of being taken for a ride, which unfortunately was a lot of the time. 'Yes, and she's not quite one. I can't imagine what the teenage years are going to be like.' She chuckled. 'Every day's exciting though.'

'I can see how much you love being a mother.' Now his steady gaze was on her, no hint of anything but respect coming her way.

'I do.' When she'd first learned she was pregnant she'd worried that she might not be any good at being a mother as she'd never had one, but she'd always known she'd give it her best shot. She had great role models in her grandparents to fall back on.

'Elyna, you're one lucky little girl.' Etienne leaned down to stand her on her feet, holding her until she had her balance. Elyna instantly plonked down on her bottom.

'Would you like some wine?' Camille asked. 'There's more of the Merlot and the Chenin Blanc we had on Sunday.'

'Thank you, I would.' He rubbed his lower back as he tried to stifle a yawn. 'Merlot, please.'

She headed for the glass cabinet. 'I've got cold chicken and salad for dinner.' Nothing fancy but easy to prepare.

Etienne straightened and stared at her. 'That's not necessary. I only came to have a talk,' he growled.

It didn't take much to get his back up. His ingrained caution was showing itself again. 'Don't worry, I'm not trying to ingratiate myself with you by making you dinner. You've been at work and will no doubt be hungry. As I need to eat I figured we might as well have a meal together. That's all.' It might also help keep things on an even keel.

He continued to watch her as she poured the wine and handed him a glass, making her wonder what was coming next. But he drew a breath, as though trying to relax, and said, 'I apologise for being rude. Dinner would be lovely, thank you.'

Phew. 'Good.' Hopefully it was another step in the right direction. Sinking onto a chair, she sipped her wine and waited. He'd come to talk, he said. Where was he going to start? Should she get things under way? Or would it be better to wait until Elyna was finally tucked up in bed? *What am I doing, waffling along in my head like this? I'm usually a lot tougher.* Yes, but she didn't want to get on the wrong side of Etienne unless she had to. He deserved better than that, and so did she. So did Elyna, for that matter. 'You are her father.'

Etienne returned to watching Elyna with the softest smile. 'She's adorable. She appears happy and healthy for being born so early. She didn't have any serious health problems?'

'There were a lot of minor infections in her lungs and mouth during the first three months. Feeding was difficult, and she had to be fed intravenously for a long while. Otherwise everything went well. Now she's so energetic it's crazy. Though she does sleep a lot,' Camille added.

He frowned. 'No long-term health problems at all?'

'The paediatricians didn't think so. I admit I'm scared to get too ecstatic in case they're wrong. I lost a lot of sleep in the first weeks of her life thinking about everything that could go wrong.'

'Were the doctors good? Knew what they were doing?'

Camille smiled. He sounded like any father she'd known. 'Relax, Etienne. They were superb. I have no complaints about how they treated Elyna. None whatsoever.'

'Just checking.' He took a big sip of his Merlot, and turned back to her. 'It's been a huge shock, but I'm sure you know that. You were right. My instant reaction was to disbelieve you. It still is. I have more questions to ask, but…' Another mouthful of wine. 'The moment I first saw Elyna I sensed something about her that I can't explain.'

Camille felt her mouth drop open. Had she heard right? This was Etienne Laval, a man who did not share personal feelings with anyone as far as she knew. That probably didn't include his own family, but still. Grappling to get her head around what he'd said, she closed her mouth and swallowed hard. Then she waited because she had no idea what to say. It would be too easy to say the wrong thing and lose ground fast.

He smiled tightly. 'If only you could see your face. Obviously it's my turn to shock you.'

He could say that again. But she wasn't asking him to. 'Can you explain more?'

'Not really. I looked at your daughter and thought she was gorgeous, and I didn't want to let you go without finding out more.'

'So that's why you insisted on giving us a ride.' Disappointment rose. She'd been silly enough to think he'd actually been pleased to see her.

'Not entirely. I offered…' He winced. 'Okay, I insisted, because I'd sometimes wondered where you'd gone, and what you'd been doing.'

He'd thought about her after she'd left the hospital? Was that a good sign? She'd thought about Etienne a lot, but then she had been carrying his baby. Truth was she'd missed him and hadn't got over him as she'd hoped. 'Now you know.'

He stood up and reached for her glass. 'Want another one?'

'I didn't realise I'd finished that one.'

'It was very small. Because you're thinking about Elyna, I take it?'

'Yes.'

'Another small one won't hurt, though maybe you could make it last a bit longer.' He gave her a light but genuine smile. 'I'm not lecturing you, Camille. I'm sure you'd never do anything to endanger your daughter.'

The way he said 'your daughter' was deliberate and firm. Still not acknowledging that Elyna was his daughter, too. Small steps, Camille thought as she rose to put the meal together, and was grateful they were getting along all right at the moment.

'So you've got a sister. Any other siblings?' Camille asked.

His face closed up.

Was there anything they could talk about without him getting upset? 'I'm sorry if I've said the wrong thing.'

'It's all right. We had a brother, Hugo. He was a year older than me. Hugo the second. Dad's the first.'

Camille's stomach scrunched in regret. She heard where this was going. 'Etienne, stop. You don't have to tell me.'

'You know what? I never talk about this and yet I find I want to tell you.'

She reached for the Merlot and topped up his glass, stunned at what he'd said. 'That means a lot.'

Etienne sipped the wine and stared at his hand. When he spoke it was so quietly she strained to hear. 'Hugo was fourteen when he had an accident on a quadbike at the vineyard. Going too fast, but he was a teenager. It's natural to think you're infallible.'

She glanced at Elyna and shivered. Who knew what lay ahead? Not that she wanted to know.

'He broke both femurs and pierced his bowel. It was an infection in his abdomen that took his life. During the operations he underwent no one noticed a second perforation of the bowel.'

'What? That's terrible.'

'Appalling.' Etienne took a deep breath and continued. 'Hugo always intended to go into the family wine business and eventually take over from Dad running the vineyards. I was meant to pick up the line after Hugo died.'

'Instead you chose medicine because of what happened to your brother?' It made perfect sense.

He nodded. 'Dad was very disappointed with me. My sister was thrilled because, like Hugo, she'd always wanted to be a viticulturist. It took some persuading to make Dad accept she was the ideal choice but they got there and now he wouldn't have it any other way. Cariole married a winemaker from Marlborough, New Zealand, and it's a perfect match in the vineyard and off it.'

'Hence your two nephews.'

'Yes.' Finally he smiled, albeit sadly. 'That's my family. We're close and there for each other during the difficult times. And the good ones,' he added more determinedly.

Family. It was all she really wanted. Camille sighed. She was a mother, but to have the other half of the picture at her side would be wonderful. It would never be Etienne. He had too much baggage to let go of before he'd ever fall in love with anyone. As for her, she still had trust issues, and even though Etienne had got to her in ways she'd never have believed, she wasn't really in love with him. She might think he was wonderful and sexy but she couldn't hand over her heart to him. He'd only give it straight back.

Placing plates and food on the table, she sat down. 'Eat and enjoy.' They didn't need any more gloomy conversation. But she would love to know what he was thinking regarding their daughter. Ask him? Or give him the space he seemed to need?

'I'm glad you took the position at Central Hospital,' he commented as he forked up chicken. 'I think you'll enjoy being back in familiar surroundings. It's one less hassle for you.'

'I hope so.' It had been too easy to give in and ignore her concerns regarding Etienne. So far she hadn't regretted her decision but then she hadn't started work properly yet. She was ready to settle down and this was another step forward. Hopefully there'd be more of those to come.

CHAPTER FOUR

'Tell me more about your family,' Etienne said on Wednesday night. Once more he was sitting at Camille's table eating a delicious meal. She certainly knew her way around a kitchen. This time he'd provided the wine, bringing one from his cellar that came from the family estate. Elyna was tucked up in bed sound asleep after he'd read her a bedtime story. Something he'd thoroughly enjoyed doing. He enjoyed being around children but under the circumstances he hadn't expected to already be quite as relaxed with Elyna as he was.

Last night he and Camille hadn't done much talking about the issue hanging between them. He'd been more intent on hearing about Elyna's birth and follow-up. There was so much he'd missed out on that a burning need to catch up took over everything else, leading to the fact he had to accept he was Elyna's father. At least they seemed to be getting on all right, but the ingrained doubt he carried remained. There was a lot to talk about before he was one hundred per cent certain where he was going with raising Elyna. Together or separately? Hence his question about her background. There were clearly some trust issues there for her as well.

She sipped her wine. 'Like I said, my grandparents raised me as my mother died two days after I was born. My mother was their only child and there was no other family to take me in.' She toyed with the glass. 'It must've been hard at times as they weren't young, but I couldn't have asked for a better upbringing.'

Unless it had been with her mother. Every child wanted to be with their parents. 'What about your father? Didn't he ever come to meet you?'

'Oh, he stepped up all right.' Bitterness tightened her face and soured her words. 'At my twentieth birthday party.'

'That was the first time you'd seen him?' This was not the story he'd expected. Camille was so balanced in her approach to life this was a shock.

'The first, not quite the last.' The level in her glass dropped as she took a large mouthful. 'It took a bit to convince him I wasn't going to hand over money every time he demanded it. He thought I owed him.'

'For what?'

'For existing.'

Etienne banged his glass down and stood to go around the table and lift Camille up into his arms for the biggest hug he had in him to give.

'Camille, you are the most amazing woman I know.' She hadn't let the low-life drag her down. She had to be strong to have managed that after waiting so long to meet him. Bet her grandparents had a lot to do with her strength.

The tension gripping her since he'd mentioned her father began to ease, her body softening in his arms. 'Thank you.'

Slowly lowering his arms, he reluctantly stepped back. Holding Camille was special. But not wise when he had no intention of getting close to her. 'I mean it.' It was the first time he'd ever said anything like that to a woman not from his family since he'd broken up with Melina.

Sinking back onto her chair, Camille lifted her glass again, then put it back down. 'I'd better go easy.'

'You've hardly touched it.' Other than that large gulp she'd taken a moment ago. 'Sit back and enjoy. Even have a refill if you'd like.' He made an instant decision, and hoped he didn't come to regret it. 'I can sleep on the couch for the night if you're worried about Elyna.'

Her reply was to blink, then take another small mouthful. Her lips lifted in a self-deprecating manner. 'I don't usually over-indulge, but thinking about that man makes me seethe.'

Returning to his seat, Etienne picked up his knife and fork and continued to enjoy the delicious casserole she'd made while listening to

Camille tell him more about the man who'd fathered her. He didn't want to stop her as he sensed she didn't talk about the subject to anyone and it might be good to get it out there for once. It was interesting that, by confiding in him like this, she made him feel closer to her in a way he hadn't expected.

'My mother met him while in Montreal visiting her uncles. From the little I've learned he was raised there. He came from a poor background but wasn't doing anything to help himself get ahead except relying on others.'

'How did you learn that?'

'I went on the Internet.'

'Of course.'

Camille placed her fork on her empty dish. 'Grandma told me that my mother refused to say anything about him even when they were dating other than to say he was a great guy.'

His mouth dried. He wished he hadn't asked about her family. It must be painful for Camille to talk about her father. He did appreciate her openness and honesty, and again he felt grateful.

'I wonder how he tracked you down.'

'No idea. He didn't say. I presume he went online too. Somehow he learned my name. I was probably vulnerable as I'd grown up wanting to know who my father was so I was open to hearing what he had to say.'

'I'm glad you had the nous to tell him where

to go.' Etienne lifted the bottle. 'Sure I can't top up your glass?'

Pushing it towards him, she gave a crooked smile. 'A very small one. Might as well add that to the list of things I'm doing tonight that I never do.'

Warmth stole through him. He was meant to be keeping his wits about him and judging how genuine she was about not demanding to be taken in along with Elyna and given a comfortable life from here on, but she undermined his determination far too easily. If he didn't over-think it, it felt wonderful she wasn't using Elyna to get something from him. He groaned internally. He was already accepting that Camille was becoming important to him, and that had nothing to do with the little girl sound asleep down the hall. Though Elyna did add to the wonderful picture of the future he was beginning to imagine. 'Does that include allowing me to sleep on the couch?'

A hint of pink touched her cheeks. 'There's a bed in the third room.'

Why did I say that? Camille asked herself silently. I mean, seriously? She wouldn't sleep a wink knowing he was just down the hall. Offering Etienne a bed meant he would stay. If he didn't stay she'd still probably lie awake all night anyway thinking about the times he'd shared a bed with her during their fling. That was one hot body under his expensive suit. A body she'd never forgotten despite everything else going on in her life. Nor had she forgotten the man behind the aloof smile. A good man with a big heart, though he didn't like to share that any more than she did hers.

'Sounds more comfortable than the couch,' he admitted, then laughed. 'I don't think I need to stay the night, though. You haven't had too much wine and Elyna's perfectly safe.'

Her heart sank with disappointment. Had she wanted him to stay? When there was so much between them that needed sorting and most likely wasn't going to be straightforward? Unfortunately she did. 'Your call.' *This is the man you started falling for, remember?* It didn't matter. She was long over that, had put him firmly aside. All that mattered now was he was Elyna's dad and they needed to work out how to go forward in a way that suited them all. Except that was a lie. Whenever he was around she got a warm sensation of something like love deep inside her heart. It made her wonder if she'd found what she'd believed she'd never want again after her disastrous relationship with Benoit.

Etienne's eyebrows rose slightly. 'I'll head home but I'd like to spend time with Elyna when possible.'

Camille felt her mouth fall open. 'Are you saying—?'

'That I believe she's my daughter?' He hesitated, as though afraid to answer. Once he put it out there, if he thought she was, then there wasn't any going back. 'I am coming to think so. Though there are things I'd like to know sooner than later. You're asking a lot of me to simply accept her as mine, yet I can't find it in me to think it's not true.'

Her head spun. She didn't begrudge him for his comment about asking a lot. But to say he believed her—because that *was* what he was saying, wasn't it?—was not what she'd been expecting so soon. He knew how to surprise her, which normally she'd find thrilling, but not when it came to Elyna's parentage. 'I'll answer your questions, but remember I've got some myself.'

His mouth tightened, but all he said was, 'I'm sure you do.'

She didn't know how to interpret that so she waited for him to go ahead.

Finally, he continued. 'Why did you break off our fling?'

She gaped at him. That was the last thing she'd expected him to ask. It had absolutely nothing to do with Elyna, and she wasn't keen to share how she'd been feeling about him at the time. Lying wasn't an option. He'd see right through her. Nor was it something she liked to do. She went for the middle road. 'It was time. I don't let any fling I'm involved in carry on for too long.'

'Why?'

'Because then it's no longer a fling but something like a relationship and I don't do those.' Damn. She'd just set herself up to be asked why not, and she wasn't exposing her gremlins over having her heart broken by the one man she had loved.

Etienne opened his mouth, closed it again. Then he nodded as though he understood where she was coming from. Which was quite possible given the way he'd spoken about past relationships to his mother that night she'd gone to tell him she was pregnant. 'You didn't want anything else from me.'

Dead right. Especially once she'd started worrying she might be falling a little in love with him. 'We got together for sex with meals often thrown in at lovely restaurants. I had a wonderful time but it couldn't go on for ever. It's not how I do these things. Not that I've had many flings.' Shut up, Camille. He didn't need to know that.

He leaned back in his chair and drained his glass. 'Let's move on before we get into a mess we can't undo.'

'Why did you go to Nice? You always said you had your dream position here in Paris.'

'I'll have another wine before I go into that one.' Etienne was off the chair and in the kitchen before he'd finished the sentence.

Camille wondered what she'd said. It had

seemed like a straightforward question but she should know better. 'It's okay. Forget I asked.'

'No, it's all right.' He sat down again and added a small amount to her glass before emptying the last of the bottle into his. 'I became restless. Everyone around me seemed to be getting their lives in order, marrying, having kids.' He shrugged too eloquently. 'I don't know. I missed you. The fact that you'd dropped by my office that night when you'd never done so before also kept nagging at me.'

She couldn't believe what she was hearing. Etienne admitted he'd missed her? No way. He couldn't have. He didn't ever get close to a woman.

He was still talking. 'I took a break and went to Nice where my friend's a partner in a surgical clinic. They needed someone to cover for another surgeon on maternity leave. Once there I thought I'd get over the restlessness, but it never wavered so at the end of my contract I returned home.'

She waited for more but it wasn't forthcoming. Etienne had said all he was going to. He'd wound her up with half a story but she wasn't letting him know that. 'Are you happy working at Central again?' she asked.

'Mostly.'

Camille stood up and collected the dishes to take to the kitchen. End of that conversation, apparently. Though it was more than she'd expected.

Etienne stood up. 'I think it's time I went. Yes, I am going home. Thank you for a delicious meal.'

'You're welcome.' Most of the time. Camille banged the plates into the dishwasher. She was being abrupt but she was suddenly impatient to know what he intended for the future. Their future regarding Elyna. His hints that he was getting there suddenly weren't enough. She needed to know. Now. But she wasn't going to beg. 'Goodnight.'

'I'm on call for the next couple of days so I might not have as much time to pop in.'

'You have my number. Any time you have something to discuss you know how to get hold of me.'

'I do.'

Suddenly Etienne was in front of her, reaching for her. His eyes were fixed on hers, watching her closely as his head lowered slowly until his lips just brushed hers. 'Camille,' he sighed as he pulled back swiftly.

Leaving her chilled and hyped all in one. 'Yes?' Had he been going to kiss her? As in a deep, heart-twisting kiss?

'Damn you, Camille. You do my head in.' His mouth suddenly covered hers, his tongue delving into her mouth, kissing her as if there were no tomorrow.

She was responding, pouring everything into their kiss, tasting him, feeling his hands on her waist, smelling his spicy scent. This was Etienne, the man breaking through her resilience, causing her to rethink not trusting her heart to anyone again. Then just as suddenly she was being put aside.

'Goodnight, Camille.' He walked away, and the main door closed quietly behind him.

All her energy drained away and she sank onto the nearest chair. 'Damn you, Etienne Laval. There are two of us trying to figure out what to do and you're not playing fair.' Not that she'd expected him to be on board straight away. In fact he was further ahead than she'd thought he'd be at this point, but it was so hard waiting for him to front up and be straightforward with her. But to kiss her as he used to? To wake her up in such a hurry she'd struggled to keep up, only to have him walk away? Goodnight, he'd said. Where did that leave her? Apart from in a right pickle of heat and longing, that was.

Tightening her arms around her upper body, she held on as if she were about to fall apart. She did care for Etienne—a little. Or a lot. She wasn't sure which. But whichever, it was enough to tip her world upside down and have her wondering if she'd made a mistake coming home and telling him about Elyna.

No, that wasn't right. Elyna would benefit from knowing her father. Her mother mightn't, but that wasn't Elyna's problem.

***

On Friday morning Camille swung Elyna up in her arms and kissed her cheeks. 'Guess what, little one? You're off to play with your new friends while Mummy goes to work.' Where she'd probably bump into Etienne at some point when he came to check up on his patients, which was the last thing she needed after that kiss. But then they had to make this work so she'd straighten her back and deal with whatever came along.

Here he comes, Camille thought as she read Bella's tympanic temperature monitor two hours later. She'd sensed his presence almost before he appeared in the doorway. Her skin had tightened and her head felt light. Toughen up, she reminded herself.

Etienne was striding towards his patient but his eyes were on her, looking surprised. 'I didn't think you were starting until Monday of next week.'

'Karina asked if I'd cover for a few hours as they're really short-staffed this morning.'

'Where's Elyna?'

'In the crèche downstairs,' she ground out. Did he think she'd left her small daughter at home alone? Of course not, but he had to know she'd make sure Elyna was sorted before she agreed to come in. 'Bella's temperature is thirty-nine point six.' He needed reminding that this wasn't the place to be discussing their daughter. Or anything personal.

He looked at her for another moment, then nodded. 'It was much the same when she was in recovery. It's not uncommon post op but keep an eye out for infection at the wound sites.' Etienne grimaced. 'Sorry, you know that.' He turned to his patient. 'The surgery went well, Bella. We removed all the lymph nodes from your left side where the cancer was, and took out the first one on the other side. The lab checked it and it's clear of cancer.'

'That's got to be good news, thank you, Doctor. I'm just glad it's all done. I don't regret having both breasts removed. It was scary waiting to get rid of the cancer. I'd hate to go through this a second time.'

As she listened, Camille slipped the pulse oximeter on Bella's finger to get a blood oxygen saturation level. 'Normal,' she told Etienne a moment later.

'Good. Have you given Bella anything for the pain since she came up from recovery?'

'That was next on my list. Though Bella's hesitant about having analgesics. She's worried she'll get too used to them.'

He turned back to his patient. 'I understand but, as I warned you before we did the procedure, you'll have some severe pain as the effects of the morphine wear off. It's better to maintain a level of painkiller that keeps the pain at bay and then wean you off.'

Bella nodded slowly. 'I have a thing about taking drugs of any kind. I'm reasonably young and fit. I can get through it all right.'

From the notes Camille knew she was thirty-three and a gym addict. 'I know what you mean about taking analgesics. The side-effects can be annoying, but it will help your recovery if you don't have too much pain over the first few days at least.' Etienne was probably about to cut her off for taking over but sometimes a nurse could get through to a patient more easily than a doctor. 'It's hard enough dealing with losing your breasts without adding severe pain to the situation.'

Bella blinked, rubbed her face. 'You're right. This is horrible. But I had to do it for my husband and kids. And me.'

Where was her husband? Camille took her hand and held it lightly. 'You'll get through this with their support.'

'I know. All right, I'll take the painkillers for now.' Suddenly Bella straightened up and plastered a smile on her tense face. 'Willem, you're here.'

A man of a similar age was crossing the room to Bella's bed, worry filling his face. 'Bella, darling, how are you?' He made to hug her, then must've realised he shouldn't and carefully sat on the edge of the bed instead.

Camille stepped away and glanced at Etienne, who was watching her, not his patient.

He nodded. Thank you, he mouthed.

A thrill ran through her. They were on track with working with patients if nothing else, and that made her hopeful they could move on from that decimating kiss. Except she already craved another one. *Stop it, Camille. Be sensible for once.* 'I'll get the tablets for Bella. I'm presuming you've signed for them.'

'You know I have.' It was said with a small smile.

This was Etienne when they'd been having a fling, warm smiles and so sexy he had her constantly wanting to get close to him. But— No, forget the buts. Let everything go. Move on. 'Just checking.' She nodded and headed away to the drugs cupboard before realising she didn't yet have access to it. It had been mayhem when she'd arrived so Karina had suggested they worry about it later when everything calmed down. 'I need someone to open the cupboard.'

'I'll do it,' Etienne said. 'But first I want to check on another patient I operated on this morning.'

'Pierre Cabot?' The sixty-four-year-old had had two hernias repaired. 'He was sleeping when I checked on him twenty minutes ago.'

'Let's hope he's awake now. The last thing I like doing is waking patients post surgery. They often tend to be grumpy.'

'That's because you're probably poking around their wound site.'

'I know. Weird, isn't it? Who'd be a doctor?' He *was* light-hearted today.

She wondered what he'd had for breakfast because she'd get in a box of it for her bleaker mornings when she worried about how they were going to manage dual parenting if—when—he came on board. *But I'm not thinking about that now.* It'd spoil the good atmosphere.

'Hey, Etienne.' Karina appeared in a doorway. 'You were right. We do need Camille back here.'

Camille turned to stare at him. 'You said that?'

'Relax. I merely reminded Karina you're an exceptional nurse.'

Whack. Her heart slammed her ribs. He'd said that? Despite their problems? Camille felt happier. 'Let's go see Pierre, and then I can give Bella some drugs before she changes her mind again.'

'Hopefully her husband will help us there,' Etienne said as they walked down the ward.

'I doubt anyone can if Bella's determined not to take them, but for now we're winning.' Taking painkillers certainly helped people through the post-surgery time when their bodies were protesting about having been cut and stitched.

Karina caught up with them. 'When you've done that take a short break, Camille. We've got more patients coming up from Theatre in about forty-five minutes.'

'Will do.'

'There's tea and coffee in the staffroom off the office,' Karina added.

'I'll just pop down and see how Elyna's doing,' Camille said.

'Fine.'

'I'll come with you,' Etienne said when Karina was out of earshot.

'Great.' Despite not giving her a definite answer he was stepping up to the father role all too easily. It was definite progress, and made her relax about everything a little more.

'It's handy having the crèche your friend manages right here in the hospital.'

'It makes life easier not having to stop off elsewhere on the way.'

'You'll be able to see her in your breaks. So will I,' he added quietly.

She further softened towards him. 'She'll like that.'

'If you need help with the fees please let me know.' When she glanced at him in surprise, he shrugged. 'I know. That's not how I usually am. But I'm getting my head around the fact that you'll probably never ask me for anything and I'd really like to share more with you than just hugging Elyna.'

Camille stopped abruptly. The man was being so open she was struggling to take it all in. 'Etienne, if you're totally on board about being her father then I'm not going to stop you being a major part of her life.'

'Except asking me for help financially.'

True. 'I am who I am.'

'Tough, independent, determined. To name a few of your better characteristics.' The smile that came with that told her he wasn't about to complain about those features.

It was a lot to take in. 'Come on. We're meant to be seeing a patient, not patting each other on the back.'

Etienne laughed, a deep, warm sound that lightened her step as she headed into the room where the patient lay sleeping. After all the tension and doubts since bumping into Etienne at Charles de Gaulle she couldn't believe how good she was feeling. And happy, because he seemed to care about her and how she was coping. No wonder those feelings of tenderness she'd felt for him during their fling were rushing back into her heart. This time she wasn't going to walk away so fast, if at all. She had to see where it led and if they didn't make it then she'd have to toughen up some more and move on. Whatever happened in the future Etienne was always going to be in her life because of their daughter.

Friday evening. It had been one of the longest weeks of his life, Etienne thought as he rang Camille's bell. Finding out he might be a father, trying to see Elyna and Camille whenever possible, a busy operating list, then being on call. He was exhausted.

'Come up,' she said when he spoke into the voice box. 'Door's open.'

She was playing with Elyna when he stepped inside the apartment. His heart expanded as he watched them, heads together, creating a structure of some sort with building blocks. Mothering came naturally to Camille. Nor had she been impatient with him as she'd waited for him to accept he was Elyna's father. How she was going to react to the invitation he was about to offer her he had no idea. It might make her pause, or she might see it as an opportunity to get closer to his family.

'Hi there, Etienne. Look who's here, Elyna.' Camille turned their girl around so she could see him.

'Hello, Elyna.' He couldn't take his eyes off the two females sneaking into his heart far quicker than he'd have believed possible. Was this why he'd mostly stayed away from flings since returning from Nice? Because Camille had already got to him in an unexpected way? Face it, even in Nice he hadn't gone looking for a bed companion more than a couple of times and those had been one-night stands. Again, he had to wonder if Camille was the reason for his abstinence. He might be accepting he was Elyna's father but to accept he was falling in love with her mother was a whole different story. One he was beginning to consider exploring. Which was huge. He'd take it slowly, because that was the only way to go and still feel in control.

'You want to hold her?' Camille asked.

Of course he did. Reaching down, he swung Elyna up into his arms and spun her around. 'Hey, little one.' Brushing a kiss on her brow, he felt his heart lift. This was what it was like to be a dad. Very damned wonderful. Glancing at Camille, he found her watching him with something like relief in those blue eyes. 'Do you still worry I might walk away from her? Because, rest assured, I will never do that.'

'I believe you, believe in you.'

Sucker-punch him, why didn't she? 'I don't know what to say to that.'

'Don't say anything, just accept it.' She looked around the room, before returning her gaze to him.

'I'll do my best.' Etienne huffed out a tight laugh. Lately his life hadn't been as devoid of excitement as usual. He'd been happy spending time at the vineyards helping his sister and brother-in-law, plus spending time with the little guys, and hadn't missed the casual affairs that had used to take up a lot of his spare time. That was when the restlessness had finally subsided. He wasn't quite where he wanted to be but at least he wasn't wasting time worrying about it any more. 'There's a lot for me to get used to. Like spending time with you both.'

Camille was gaping at him, slightly stunned.

He chuckled. 'It is possible for me to lead a quiet life, you know.'

Her mouth tipped up into one of those bright smiles that twisted his heart. 'No, I didn't know you could manage that.'

Nor had he, until this particular woman got under his skin and harassed him with images of her smiling and laughing and groaning with sexual pleasure when they'd made love. It had been more than just sex towards the end, and one reason he'd been somewhat relieved she'd pulled away. Then there'd been all the reasons he'd wished she hadn't. 'Guess there's a lot for you to learn about me, going forward.' He had a plan for getting that under way very soon that he'd put to her shortly.

'Down,' Elyna cried, wriggling in his arms.

'Sure thing, little one.' He set her on her feet, holding her until she had her balance, which lasted all of five seconds. 'You certainly know what you want, don't you?'

'She was born like that,' Camille commented in a loving voice.

If only she could speak to him in the same way. Another thing he'd have to work on if he wanted more than a platonic relationship with her. Did he? Or didn't he? A huge question and one he wasn't prepared to answer yet, maybe never. 'But she was premature.'

'It was obvious from the get-go that she had a determined nature. No giving up even on the less than easy days.'

'How did that make you feel?' He'd bet his career that Camille would've been as determined as her daughter.

'Hopeful, and in sync with her.'

'I wish I'd been there for you both.' It was true. He struggled with what he'd missed because he hadn't known Camille was having his child. 'I'm not looking for trouble and trying to blame you,' he added hurriedly.

'If it's any comfort, I'd have liked having you there. There were days in the first weeks that I despaired of Elyna making it through the horror of being wired to every machine imaginable that did everything for her.'

He stepped close to place an arm around her shoulders. There was a light quiver going on under his hand. 'For what it's worth, Elyna doesn't look any the worse for her early start in life.' His hand tightened around her before he remembered what he was going to ask later and dropped his arm to put some space between them. 'Can I ask what you've got planned for the weekend?' Hopefully nothing important. He wanted time with Elyna to start making up on what he'd already missed out on.

'Topping up the pantry, taking Elyna for walks in the park, not much else.'

'Then how about you join me for lunch tomorrow? At my house,' he added so she understood that he was opening up more of his life to her. But that was only the beginning. His chest rose as he drew a breath. 'My parents will be there. They are dying to meet you and Elyna.'

Camille's mouth fell open. 'What?'

'I've told them about Elyna. It had to happen and I figured the sooner they knew, the sooner we could make some plans for the future. Besides, why shouldn't they know they've got a granddaughter?'

'Of course it's the right thing to do. Because you haven't straight out said you accept Elyna's your daughter, I hadn't expected you to have talked to them already. But then, why wouldn't you have? Are they all right with the news?'

'Beyond all right. Mum can't wait to hold Elyna and hug her. I warn you, she can be a bit OTT when it comes to her grandchildren.'

Doubt was settling over Camille's face.

'You'll be fine, Camille. They want to get to know you too. They won't put you through the mill with a million questions. I'd stop them if they did but it won't happen.'

Her face didn't clear. Instead she shrugged.

'I've known this day would come, but it's going to be hard.'

'So you'll come to lunch?'

'Yes.'

'I'll pick you up at eleven.'

'We'll be ready. How about a glass of wine?' she asked.

'I'll get it.'

Camille watched Etienne walk through to the kitchen as though he didn't have a care in the world. If only she felt half as confident. She was meeting his parents. Tomorrow. They'd know that she hadn't told Etienne she was pregnant before leaving Paris to go to Montreal.

'This day was always going to come,' she muttered. But she was no more prepared for it now that Etienne accepted Elyna was his than she'd been at any time since seeing her positive HCG result. 'Time to suck it up and get on with reality.'

If only tomorrow were a few weeks away. More time to allow her to get used to the idea of fronting up to Etienne's parents might help. Or not. It wasn't as though this were happening within days of Elyna being born. She'd spent many hours thinking about Etienne's parents and how they'd react to the news they had a granddaughter. Anyway, since when had she become a coward? Etienne had surprised her in more ways than one.

His acceptance of Elyna had been easier than she'd thought possible. The fact he was taking her to his house tomorrow was unexpected. She didn't think they were that far into this parenting relationship for that.

This time tomorrow she'd know a bit more about Etienne's family, which had to be good. Fingers crossed. Etienne seemed to have a solid relationship with them so it would be strange if they didn't reach out to their grandchildren. She wanted Elyna to have wonderful grandparents willing to be there for her whenever needed as hers had been for her. It was hideous imagining how her life might've turned out if not for them. At least Elyna had a father who wasn't denying his role, just taking time to accept it completely, which was way more than she'd had.

'Up, Mama. Up.' Elyna stood before her, stretching her arms up. 'Up.'

Swinging her into her arms and hugging her against her chest, Camille blinked as sudden tears appeared at the corners of her eyes. 'I'm so lucky to have you, sweetheart. So is your daddy.' He just had to learn how lucky. Or did he already know?

Etienne brought the wine through, suddenly looking tense. Camille watched him close the curtains in the lounge. He'd been relaxed only moments before. 'Everything all right?'

'Why wouldn't it be?' He pulled a chair around to face her and sank down, his elbows on his knees.

She wasn't going there. Instead she'd wait him out because in the end he would speak his mind. He wasn't one to hold back when it was important.

As the silence grew deafening she began to squirm. Should she say something? Ask what was bothering him? Then it hit her. He wanted Elyna. Inviting her to his place was the first step to upping the ante. He was going to make it difficult for her to keep her daughter. 'Etienne.' She stopped. What to say without sounding desperate? And doing that wouldn't help her side of the story.

'Relax, Camille. We need to find a way for both of us to be with Elyna as much as possible. I don't want to only be a drop-in dad. I want to be fully involved in her life.'

'I agree.'

He went quiet again. Where was this going? 'I have something to ask you.' He paused, staring at the floor between his legs before he then lifted his head and fixed a steady gaze on her. 'Will you marry me?'

He could have knocked her down with a feather! That was the last thing she'd expected. 'Did you just say what I think you did?'

'I asked you to marry me, Camille. That way we can raise Elyna together, share a home, be a family.'

What about love? What about more children? What about sharing their lives completely? No, this wasn't about them. It was only about their daughter. She couldn't, wouldn't, do it. Not even for Elyna because, in the end, without love it wouldn't work for any of them. She stood up, unable to sit still a moment longer. 'I hear where you're coming from, Etienne.' She paused. Took a deep breath. 'But my answer is no, I will not marry you.'

His head jerked back. His eyes were wide with shock. He'd really believed she'd say yes!

That hurt. Big time. She was not like the other women he'd had in his life. This might be about Elyna but he'd still believed she'd grab the opportunity and say yes so all her problems would be solved. 'I won't marry you because to me marriage is purely about love. Without that it's hollow. I won't do it.'

He stood up slowly and came to take her hands in his. For once, they didn't feel soft and warm, but chilly and rigid. 'I think you're wrong. No, we're not in love, but we get along well, and I believe we would grow together over time.'

Pulling away from him, she gazed into his lovely grey eyes and tried to keep her head on straight. It wasn't easy because he already meant so much to her. Enough that she suspected she might already be on the way to loving him. She accepted that, but it didn't make saying yes to his proposal right. She hadn't completely lost her head over him yet. Anyway there was no suggestion he might feel the same about her. 'That isn't how I perceive a successful marriage to be. I don't believe you do either. You're trying to do the right thing by your child, but, Etienne, it won't work.'

'The one thing I've always said about you from the first time we got together is that you can be brutally honest.'

'I'm not going to change.'

'I wouldn't expect you to. Or want you to.' He moved away. 'I'm sorry you don't see my proposal as being the best solution for us all.'

So was she. More than sorry. How ironic that Etienne wanted her to accept his offer for all the wrong reasons. 'I'm sorry, Etienne, but I won't change my mind.'

He came over and placed a light kiss on her cheek. 'We'll see about that. See you tomorrow.' Then he was gone, leaving a challenge hanging in the air.

We'll see about that.

Etienne had asked her to marry him. But he didn't love her. She shivered. What could be worse than a loveless marriage? Or one where she loved him and he didn't reciprocate her feelings?

A tear snuck down her cheek where he'd kissed her. She'd thought a proposal was the ultimate dream but not in this case. So close yet so far.

CHAPTER FIVE

'I HAVEN'T ASKED where you live,' Camille said as Etienne manoeuvred through the Saturday traffic on the way to his house.

'Rambouilet,' he told her, surprised she hadn't looked it up. But then Camille didn't seem to spend all her time finding out everything possible about him or his family. 'Near the Versailles Palace,' he added in case she didn't know. He was still trying to accept she'd turned his proposal down.

'I had a friend who boarded in that area while doing her nursing training. It's lovely.'

He glanced sideways to see if her face had lit up in anticipation, but no, she looked the same as she had since he'd picked her up. Tense and worried, even a little angry. 'Camille, everything's going to be all right.' With his parents anyway. 'I haven't mentioned to them that I asked you to marry me.' He was determined not to get into an argument with her about Elyna either. They'd done pretty well so far, and long may that continue for everyone's sakes.

She softened a little. 'Thanks.'

'But?'

She huffed out a breath. 'I do feel guilty about not telling you earlier, no matter what the reasons, which means your parents also missed out on Elyna's first year.'

He could agree with her, but in the end what'd happened couldn't be undone so he might as well let it go once and for ever. He wanted to get on well with Camille, not become awkward and guarded around her, and maybe one day she'd change her mind about marrying him so they could co-parent their child better. For that to happen he needed to stop kissing her as he had the other night. That kiss had messed with his mind ever since. He wanted more but was going to resist.

'I've explained to my family what went down and why and no one's raised any doubts so you can put it behind you. We might be coming at this from different perspectives but we're in it together, Camille.' He meant it. Making a happy life and home for Elyna was important, and so was co operating with Camille. If she'd let him in, that was, and hopefully his plans would see to that despite the kiss. It had been a mistake he couldn't afford to repeat.

She turned in her seat to regard him thoughtfully. 'Until last night you've been good about everything. I know there've been times when you wanted to spit out what you really thought of me.'

His chest tightened. Only Camille would say that. Just as only Camille got to him in an unprecedented manner. 'Have you always been so honest when it comes to saying how you feel?'

'Probably not always, but most of the time, sure. My grandparents never hid anything from me about my mother and that helped me growing up. Right from the first time I asked about my father they told me they knew nothing about him. While that was hard to take I learned to be as honest as them. It doesn't always win me any favours,' she said with a small smile.

'Don't change on my account. It's refreshing.'

'I'll do my best,' she agreed, relaxing further.

'That's all I expect.' Damn, he needed to relax too or lunch would be a failure, something he didn't want, though, knowing his mother, it would go well no matter what. She was excited about meeting Camille and Elyna. 'Did I tell you Mum's thrilled you've given Elyna her mother-in-law's name?'

'I'm pleased she's okay with it. Apart from being a family name, it's pretty.'

Etienne smiled internally. He had to agree. Not only the name but the wee girl who had been given it was also pretty, just like her mother. When was he going to stop thinking about Camille in that way? She was his daughter's mother, not his lover. Or the love of his life.

Turning into his driveway, he pulled up beside his father's vehicle and sighed. Home sweet home. He enjoyed living here, even though it did get lonely at times. Hopefully that would change in some ways. He was about to let Camille and Elyna into his home, and maybe fully into his heart, though that could take a lot longer. Not so much with Elyna. She was there already. It was harder with Camille. Old fears were difficult to ignore.

She was staring around at his home and the beautiful gardens surrounding it. Amazement filled her eyes as she turned to him. 'This is spectacular.'

He nodded. 'I was very lucky to have inherited the property from my grandfather. His gardener's grandson is my gardener, which is a real bonus otherwise you'd be looking at a shambles of long grass with no flowers and shrubs.'

'I doubt that very much,' Camille retorted around a smile. 'You'd never let that happen.'

She was right. He wouldn't. But he appreciated that she believed it of him. Suddenly he was nervous, an unusual sensation. This was going to be all right, wasn't it? Camille wouldn't walk out in a huff if someone said the wrong thing? She was struggling but surely she wouldn't become difficult with his parents and deny them access to

Elyna? No, that was one thing he could be certain about: she wanted Elyna to know her only grandparents because of how close she'd been to hers.

He'd have to wait and see how any other concerns played out. No point in second-guessing. His stomach was tight. Camille had knocked at his certainties and made him wonder where he was at—like how often the thought of love crossed his mind and heart when he was with her. That had nothing to do with Elyna. She was a separate matter. Her mother was his biggest concern at the moment.

'Come on, let's go inside.' He needed to get the introductions out of the way. Then hopefully everyone would relax a little. His mother was worried Camille mightn't take to the family in an open, caring way. His father was more concerned about what she might be after, as he'd been for a while, but now believed he'd been wrong to think that.

Going around to the other side of the car, he opened the back door and unclipped Elyna's safety belts before lifting her into his arms. 'Hey, little one. You're about to meet your grandparents.'

Camille stared at him. 'You do totally believe me.'

His stomach dropped. He hadn't actually put it into words for her yet. 'Yes, Camille, I do, otherwise we wouldn't be doing this.'

'Thank you. I wanted to believe that was why you suggested this, and the reason behind your proposal, but a part of me struggles with you accepting the truth after whatever's happened to you in the past, which I still know nothing about.'

He closed the door, and started walking towards the main entrance. 'My ex-fiancée told me she was pregnant when I broke up with her. I'd overheard some rather brutal comments from her to a friend, about her plans for our future. The pregnancy was a lie, designed to get me to reconsider calling off our marriage.'

'No wonder you made that comment the night I came to see you.' A warm hand touched his back. 'There are some selfish people out there.' Her tight voice suggested she'd also had her share of being mistreated by someone special. He wondered who it might have been.

'Come inside and meet two people who're nothing like that.' His steps were lighter as he walked beside Camille. She hadn't said he was an idiot to believe other women would do what Melina had, and that she'd never do something like that. She'd just accepted what he'd told her and understood his pain. With his hand on the door, he hesitated. 'Camille, are you all right with this? I know it's not easy for you, but I've got your back. Not that you'll need me, but I understand if you're nervous.' If he was nervous then she was probably falling off the edge even though she was one strong lady.

She blinked at him. 'I'll be fine.' Strong words, but not quite the strongest he'd ever heard her speak.

Placing his hand on her elbow, he led her inside and through to the cosy family room where the fire was blazing, emitting warmth they both needed right now. 'Mum, Dad, I'd like you to meet Camille Beauregard.' He meant it. Not only did he want them to meet her, he longed for them to like her—a lot.

'Camille, I've been watching the clock constantly from the moment Etienne left to collect you both.' His mother rushed at Camille and wrapped her in a hug. 'I'm Louise, by the way.' She pulled back a little. 'And this gorgeous man is Etienne's father, Hugo.'

Camille looked a bit stunned at being held so tight by the woman she'd been worried about meeting.

Etienne smiled. That was his mother to a T.

Camille looked across to his father. 'Hello, Hugo. It is good to meet you both. I've been looking forward to this day for a while.'

Dad nodded. 'I'm glad you're here, Camille. We both are.'

In Etienne's arms, Elyna began wriggling to be let down. 'Hang on, little one, not so fast. There are some people longing to meet you.'

***

Camille stepped back from Etienne's mother and drew a breath. She hadn't expected to be hugged, and she felt a lot better about introducing Elyna to her grandparents now. She reached for Elyna, taking her from her father and holding her out to Louise, her heart thumping so loudly everyone must've heard it. 'Louise, Hugo, this is your granddaughter, Elyna.'

Tears competed with a huge smile on Louise's face as she tentatively took Elyna in her arms. 'Hello, sweetheart. You're gorgeous, aren't you?'

Stepping back, Camille bumped up against Etienne and felt his arm go around her waist. His strength supported her, gave her more confidence. So far everything was going well, but that didn't stop her knees knocking. Meeting Etienne's parents and introducing Elyna to them was huge. She couldn't believe they were here doing this. She needed to relax and go with the flow. Leaning her head against Etienne's shoulder, she watched Elyna studying her grandmother with a smile growing larger by the minute. 'At least she's not screaming the house down,' Camille murmured.

'She readily accepts strangers, doesn't she? She didn't back off from me the first time we met either.'

Camille shuddered. 'As I said before, I'll have to focus on teaching her not to talk to strangers.'

Etienne laughed softly. 'Can you wait for a year or two? I know what you mean though. It's scary even thinking about it.' Father to the fore.

She liked that. He was good with Elyna but that had never been one of her concerns. They'd resolved the biggest one. He'd finally fully accepted he was her father. His parents certainly had. The joy on their faces was heart-warming. It made her happy. So far so good. Too good? Cynic. Ouch. Wasn't that what Etienne called himself that night at his office? Were they more alike than she'd realised? 'I imagine there'll be lots of things to worry about over the next fifty years,' she murmured.

Another laugh. 'Only fifty?'

'Once a parent, always a parent,' Louise said as she passed Elyna to Hugo.

So much for thinking she and Etienne were talking between themselves. Of course they were in a small area and everything could be heard. 'When did you last tell Etienne not to talk to strangers?'

Hugo answered before Louise could say a word. 'When he told me I didn't know what I was talking about. He was about nineteen at the time,' Hugo added with a grin.

A laugh bubbled out of Camille's throat. 'That old?'

'I know. You'd have thought he was only three.'

'Here's hoping his daughter's more cautious.

So far I'm not sure who she takes after the most. She does like wearing pink, which I doubt has ever been Etienne's preference,' Camille teased.

'There was one time...' Hugo stopped and laughed. 'You want to get down, don't you, missy?' Placing Elyna on her bottom, he watched her start to charge around the room inspecting everything she came across.

Glancing at Etienne, Camille saw him grinning as though he was happy to see her getting along with his father. It wasn't hard to do. Both Hugo and Louise hadn't made her feel out of place at all.

Louise followed Elyna as though she didn't want to leave her. She looked smitten.

'I think we should have a glass of wine before lunch,' Etienne announced. 'Nothing unusual about that in this family, Camille.'

So she'd gathered over the past week with Etienne's regular, albeit brief, visits, due to him being on call. 'As long as you don't intend starting Elyna on wine tasting yet I'm happy.'

'What would you like? There's quite a variety to choose from. All made on the family estate, of course.' The pride in his face made her understand how this family stuck together through everything.

'I'd like a white, but I'll let you select which one.' She wasn't going to be presumptuous and make a choice when her wine-tasting skills came down to either liking it or not.

'While you're pouring the wine I'll check on lunch,' Louise said. 'I hope you like duck à l'orange, Camille.'

'It's one of my favourite meals.'

'Come and chat while I attend to the duck.' She sounded friendly but Camille found herself wondering if this was when the questions began.

It had to happen and the sooner they were out of the way, the better. 'Sure. Anything I can do to help?'

'Not a thing. I know what it's like when you've got a little one to take care of. Never a spare moment.'

'True, but I love it. I never quite expected raising a child to be so hard and yet so much fun. I must've been in la-la land.'

'And you're doing it on your own.'

Was that a question in disguise? 'So far, yes, but I have absolutely no regrets.' Wrong, there had been. 'What I meant was that I don't regret being on my own. I do regret not telling Etienne before I left for Montreal.'

Turning to face her, Louise leant back against the high-end bench top and locked a formidable gaze on her. 'What happened can't be undone, Camille. There were two of you there that night and after Etienne told me what had happened

I think he has to own some of it too. I've told him so.'

Wow. Really? 'Thank you. Etienne has told me he does feel that way.'

'Then there's nothing to worry about, is there?'

Only what happens next. 'It was good to clear the air.'

'You two have a lot of decisions to make. Don't rush. A mistake now could take its toll on Elyna in the future.'

'I agree.' Camille sighed. If Louise weren't Etienne's mother she might want to have an in-depth conversation about what to do going forward. Louise didn't appear to be pushy or demanding, and only wanted what was best for her granddaughter, and no doubt her son when it came down to it.

Etienne appeared, carrying two glasses of wine. 'Here you go. Try this one, Camille. It's our Chardonnay.' He knew it was her favourite choice.

'Thanks.' She sipped it and blinked. 'That's beautiful.' She tried another sip. 'But then I am an amateur when it comes to varietals.' She'd drunk enough in her time but had never got invested in the subtleties of wines. Maybe it was time to start. 'Explain the flavours to me.'

Louise rolled her eyes. 'Not if we're going to eat lunch on time.'

Etienne laughed. 'We'll save it for another day.'

'Good. Then I won't reveal my lack of knowledge to everyone.' So there would be more days together. She'd known that was going to happen but wasn't sure how close they'd get after last night. It was meant to be all about Elyna and nothing to do with the increasing sense of longing for Etienne in her heart. To think she'd walked away from him when she'd been in the midst of an amazing fling. Now she'd turned down his proposal. But saving her heart came first. So would she put as much distance between them again? Not possible when Elyna was the reason for seeing so much of him. That would not be right. Elyna came first. But her heart was a close second.

'The duck's ready, Camille. What about Elyna? I take it you brought food for her?'

'Yes, it's in the chilly bag. I'll get a plate to put it on, if that's all right?'

'Camille.' Etienne sounded stern. 'You don't have to ask permission to use anything around here. Just do whatever you want.' He took a step towards the bag she'd mentioned, and paused to look at her. Then he picked it up, looking perplexed, before opening it.

Was that because he wasn't used to having to say that to the women he brought here? More likely others made the most of being in his territory and not holding back when they wanted something. *Well, Etienne, I'm not going to charge around as though I have every right to be here.* Because she didn't. He might be her daughter's father but that didn't give her leeway to make herself at home. 'Elyna's lunch is in that pink container. It's an assortment of fruit and snacks.'

'It looks good,' Etienne said as he headed to a floor-to-ceiling cupboard and got a plate. 'I've put a high chair in the dining room. It's the one I used when my nephews were Elyna's age.'

'You're right at home with little ones,' Camille noted. He'd been on the ball from the moment he first met Elyna. 'Are you going to supervise her meal?'

'You bet.' Then he looked around. 'Unless you want to, Mum?'

There was longing in Louise's eyes but she shook her head. 'No, that's your job, Etienne. What's Hugo up to?' She disappeared out of the kitchen in a rush.

Etienne looked gobsmacked. 'She's trying to stir things up.'

'She's supporting you,' Camille said around the lump forming in her throat. It'd been a while since she'd had her grandmother to do that for her and suddenly she missed her and Grandpa so much that pain crashed into her chest. They'd supported her throughout her life, and when she'd told Grandma she was pregnant her news had been welcomed, not turned into something negative.

Most of all she missed the easy love that had always come her way from her small family. The love she'd believed Benoit had felt for her had turned out to be false and the experience had put her on alert when it came to sharing her heart again. But more and more she wanted to try, to take a risk and possibly find true happiness. Her eyes went to Etienne placing his daughter in the high chair. Could he be the one? She'd certainly never felt so light and hopeful with any other man since Benoit. She believed she could trust Etienne, that if he gave his word he'd stick to it. He wouldn't lie about important things, or indeed anything at all. But, she warned herself, she'd believed that once before.

Pulling out a stool from the island in the centre of the kitchen, she sat to watch Etienne and Elyna, and her heart swooped like a bird on a breeze. They were perfect together. Right from the first time she saw him, Elyna had accepted her father as if he'd always been in her life. Etienne hadn't really backed off all that much either. He'd been shocked, wary and angry but he hadn't out and out accused her of lying to him, which was huge after the way he'd been treated in the past.

'They look good together,' Louise said quietly from behind her.

Spinning around, Camille nearly fell off the stool. 'You're right. They do.'

'I've got something to show you,' Louise told her as she dug into her enormous handbag. 'This is Hugo's mother when she was about Elyna's age.' She handed over a photograph of a little girl in a white dress sitting on a high-backed chair.

Camille stared at the photo. 'I thought Elyna looked like my grandmother, but they could be the same girl, they're so alike.' If ever proof of paternity was needed, this was it, but she wasn't about to say so. That would be tacky. Reaching for her wine, she took a mouth-watering sip, without tasting anything. 'Unreal.'

'You know Elyna was my mother's name, not Louise's, don't you?' Hugo stood beside Louise watching her. He obviously hadn't heard what Louise had just said.

'Yes, I did.' Was that a problem for Hugo?

He stared at her for a moment, then smiled. 'Thank you. I'm pleased you chose it. It's good to keep the name in the family, and it's beautiful.'

All the air gushed out of her lungs. Hugo had just said he approved of her.

Then she felt Etienne's hand on her shoulder, giving her a small squeeze. 'There you go. Elyna has grandparents.'

Camille's eyes closed as she tried to take everything in. She'd come here today expecting a grilling, and instead had been accepted for her role in this family. The words slipped out without thought. 'Thank you all so much.'

***

Etienne couldn't stop the banging going on in his chest. Even removing his hand from Camille's warm shoulder didn't calm his heart. She was turning out to be one amazing woman. As if he didn't already know. Yes, well, maybe he did.

He returned to the other delightful female in his life. 'Hey, little one. You've finished all that food already?' Obviously making up for a slow start to life. It was hard to picture her at birth, weighing only two kilos, attached to every imaginable tube and monitor, fighting to survive. Now she wore a perpetual smile and giggled a lot, sneaking into his heart far too easily. As her mother had a way of doing. Lifting Elyna out of the high chair, he placed her on the floor, where she immediately headed for the boys' toybox he'd brought out last night.

'Lunch smells delicious,' Camille remarked, walking past carrying a platter with the duck à l'orange.

'It'll taste even better.' His mother knew how to put a great meal together. He was lucky with his parents. They had been there for him and his sister growing up, and when they'd lost his brother they'd suffered deeply but had still managed to help him and Cariole cope with their grief. Camille had missed out on having parents. Though her grandparents had been wonderful she'd admitted to feeling a loss by not having her mother around. She didn't say that about her father.

He pulled out a chair for her, then went to get the wine to replenish everyone's glasses before sitting down beside her. 'You feeling comfortable?'

'Yes, I am. More than I'd thought I would.'

'Would you like to stay the night? You'd have your own room.' *Unfortunately*, his mind threw back at him, along with images of her stunning body curled around him as they got their breath back after another round of amazing sex. 'There's a cot for Elyna. We could spend more time getting to know each other better, which is important if we're going to make life easy for her.' Forget sex. As wonderful as it had been, it would get in the way of sensible decisions about where to go from here with Elyna.

Her eyes widened, and she looked thoughtful. 'I didn't come prepared for that.'

'Most things you require are here, except for clothes, which I guess is probably the most important,' he said with a grin. 'There are shops a couple of streets away if necessary.'

Her hair swung side to side as she shook her head. 'No, I can't.' She paused and stared at her fingers as though the answer to his invitation was there. Then she looked up and he knew he wouldn't be having house guests that night. 'Can

I take a rain check? I haven't come prepared with food and clothes for Elyna either.'

'It can be sorted easily enough.' It stung that she hadn't leapt for joy at his invitation, but again, this was Camille. When was he going to learn to accept her independent ways?

'Etienne, I'm not saying no for ever, only tonight. It's already been a big day for me, and Elyna. I didn't sleep much last night for worrying about how your family would react to me. I'd like to be at home tonight where I feel comfortable.'

He had to go along with that even if it seemed as though she was looking for an excuse not to stay. 'No problem. How about I show you around my home later when Elyna's taking a nap?' Then she'd understand how spacious the place was and see that they could live here in the future without bumping into each other at every turn.

Relief filled her face. 'I'd like that. From what I've seen so far it's a beautiful home.'

'It is.' At least he'd won that one. Camille would do just about anything to make sure Elyna knew her family and that they had a part in her life but she would also take care of herself so that Elyna didn't suffer from any mistakes they might make on this strange journey. 'Good. Now let's enjoy lunch. Mum, do you need a hand with something?' She and Dad were taking their time in the kitchen.

'No, thanks. We're coming. Hugo's just opening a bottle of champagne.'

He'd bet they were deliberately giving him and Camille some space. 'My family use any occasion to have champagne. Hope you like it?'

Her tongue did a lap of her lips. 'I love it. That's one wine I'm picky about and I know I'm about to have one I'll really enjoy.'

'So much for the Chardonnay.' He hadn't filled the glasses yet, so no loss.

'Here we go.' Dad placed glasses of champagne at each setting.

Etienne waited till his parents were seated then raised his glass. 'To a great lunch.'

Camille nodded as she lifted her glass. The smile she gave him turned his head and put his heart further out of whack. He was so not ready for this. If he kept telling himself that, then finally he'd have to believe it. Wouldn't he? What if he didn't want to? What if he truly was falling for Camille and wanted the whole caboodle?

And now he was supposed to eat lunch with that question banging around in his skull?

CHAPTER SIX

ETIENNE SLIPPED THE taxi driver more than enough for the fare, before brushing a kiss on Elyna's cheek. 'Goodnight, sweetheart.' If only he could do the same to Camille, but he didn't need a slap across the face. It'd be a verbal one, but still. If only she'd agreed to stay over they could've gone down the road for breakfast, then taken Elyna to the park, doing the things families did on a Sunday morning. Being turned down—again—had hurt. Again. Considering he always expected to be used, it surprised him when Camille didn't.

'Goodnight, Etienne,' the woman toying with his sanity called quietly as she slid into the back of the taxi beside Elyna. At least it was goodnight, not goodbye.

He strode around and grabbed her door before it closed. Leaning in, he said, 'Sleep tight.' He wasn't going to. Images of that sexy body had been hassling him, knocking him off centre ever since he'd picked her up that morning. They weren't likely to disappear just because he needed some sleep. Not when those figure-hugging jeans and the aqua-coloured merino polo-neck jersey that accentuated her full breasts and narrow waist kept reminding him of the feel of her warm, satin skin as he'd made love to her. It wasn't as if that had happened yesterday, yet he still had clear, vivid memories of their nights together!

'Absolutely.' She made to pull the door closed and this time he let it go.

'See you soon,' he called as the taxi pulled away. 'Because we have an issue to resolve and it isn't Elyna.' It did include their daughter, but right now all his heart was concerned about was getting closer to the woman who'd borne him a child and gave him a fierce hope that he might find a happy life in the not too distant future.

Back inside, he poured a brandy and downed a mouthful before going to his office where a firebox gave out welcoming heat. Settling into his leather lounge chair, he stretched his legs out in front of him and leaned his head back.

'What a week. And to top it off, Camille turned my proposal down.' It still rattled him. He couldn't recall a woman who'd have done that. He'd spent his whole life aware of people who wanted to be his friend, his lover, his wife all because of his wealth. Fortunately he did have genuine friends who liked him for himself. Those he treasured. Then along came Camille and tipped his thinking upside down. She'd said no. She didn't want to marry him. As plain as it could get. Thinking about it, her answer hadn't been totally out of the blue. He should be grateful she wasn't out to grab all she could, yet he was privately peeved that she hadn't said yes.

His ego had been bruised and he wasn't used to it. *Get over yourself, man. Stop feeling sorry for yourself.* Was that what this feeling was? Had he expected Camille to drop to her knees with gratitude over his proposal? And when she hadn't, had he not been able to believe her reaction because no one else would have refused him?

He got up to pace the room. He wasn't liking what he was seeing about himself almost more than he didn't like Camille's rejection.

Did her refusal to marry him mean she didn't have any feelings for him at all? Other than as a colleague and possibly a friend sharing their daughter's upbringing? There'd been moments when he'd caught her looking at him with what he'd thought was longing. But he'd often been wrong when it came to reading Camille so what was to say he was right about that?

Camille wanted love. Believed in love when it came to a permanent relationship and marriage. She wanted to love her husband and be loved in return. She'd get no argument from him. That was the golden dream. A loving, happy, sharing marriage with two people raising their children together. The problem being he couldn't give her that. No damned way. No one was getting the opportunity to undermine his love if he got that far. No one. His heart was tough now, stronger for the ugly lessons it had learned. There'd be no stepping away from that and trying again however much he wanted to.

Pausing to pick up his glass, he took another mouthful of brandy and then twirled the glass in his fingers. Was his shock and disappointment over Camille saying no really only because his pride had taken a hit? Or did it have something to do with the whirling emotions that filled him whenever he was with her? Did he actually love her or mainly feel comfortable around her because she made no demands on him?

Time to be ruthlessly honest. He did have feelings for Camille. Feelings that grew stronger by the day but that he didn't want to be feeling at all. Every time he saw her his heart lit up, his steps were lighter. She snagged his attention without trying. So what was next? Staying safe was his only option. Which meant not getting too close. Already he knew keeping his distance would be difficult, but a lot less likely to decimate him than it would be if he pursued her. He'd never do that. But he had to accept they'd spend a fair amount of time together because of Elyna. The sooner he got onto sorting out sharing the raising of her, the better, then he'd see less of Camille and be able to get firmly back on track with his life of family and medicine, and now Elyna. He didn't need anything more to keep his feet firmly on the ground. Certainly not a beautiful, caring, understanding woman who'd never take the easy way out of a conundrum.

'It's barely gone six o'clock,' Camille groaned the next morning as she clambered out of bed after a sleepless night to pick Elyna up out of her cot. Her head was full of fog and her body ached in every place imaginable. 'Damn you, Etienne Laval. I need my sleep now I've got Elyna to take care of. Lots of it.'

'Mama, up. Up,' Elyna squealed. 'Up.'

Lifting her up, Camille said, 'You're so lucky to have your daddy.'

Guilt raised its head once more. She hadn't known her father but Elyna had already spent time with hers. She'd missed out on the first eleven months of her life with him but going forward the future looked good. It would not be the same as sharing a home with him, or having a proper family where eating meals around the table at the end of a busy day talking about what they'd done was the norm. She couldn't help that. She was not marrying Etienne. He didn't love her and that was the bottom line as far as she was concerned. She'd known a caring, loving childhood with her grandparents and Elyna wasn't getting any less, only in a different way.

'Mama,' Elyna squealed. 'Hungry.' Her little face was red with effort.

Or was it something else? The nurse inside her kicked in. 'Elyna? Are you all right? Not sick?' Laying her hand on Elyna's forehead, she sighed with relief. No excessive heat there. But what about her stomach? Gently pressing Elyna's abdomen got her a whack on the shoulder with a tiny fist but no cries of pain.

'Brekfa. Now.'

Brekfa? A new word. Woohoo! Spinning Elyna around, she kissed her cheek. 'You're amazing. I'm guessing brekfa means breakfast.' Time for coffee too, now she was out of bed. There wouldn't be a chance to sneak back under the covers for a few more minutes of peace and quiet. Besides, with Etienne appearing in her head almost nonstop last night, she knew there was no chance of any peaceful moments even if Elyna managed to entertain herself.

Opening the blinds in the kitchen, she noted the clear sky. Winter put on some great days. She made an instant decision. 'Come on, we'll have a shower and go for a nice Sunday breakfast down the road at the café by the supermarket.' Then they'd go for a walk along the Seine. The thought of fresh air and not wondering if Etienne was about to ring her doorbell lifted her spirits a little. As if he would. He wouldn't come begging. Truth was she really had no idea what he'd do.

He'd asked her to marry him out of the blue.

Her heart had dropped then and was doing so now as the memory ran through her mind. In other circumstances she might've said yes. Those circumstances being that he loved her and couldn't imagine living without her. But he didn't. He'd proposed for Elyna's sake, not hers. Not theirs.

Her phone played a tune.

Etienne? If so, she'd ignore it. Right now he was the last person she wanted to talk to. She'd spent half the night having one-sided conversations with him. She didn't need any more.

Liza's name was on the screen. Early for her.

'Hi, Liza. What's up?'

'I'm in town for the day. Problems with my staff. Feel like catching up?'

Perfect. That'd be a reason not to talk to Etienne. 'Definitely.'

'Great. What time and whereabouts?'

'I was planning on going for breakfast along the road shortly but can put it off for an hour or two if you want to join us.'

'Give me an hour and I'll meet you wherever you intend going.'

After giving Liza the name of the café, Camille made her first coffee of the day and heated up some oatmeal for Elyna to get through the next hour or so. So much for Liza having a break for the first time in years. It must be a big problem for her to come back from Marseilles for a day.

Ninety minutes later she had Elyna in a high chair and was pulling out a seat at the table she'd selected away from too many people.

'Hi there.' Liza rushed up and wrapped her arms around Camille.

They held on tight for a long moment before Liza turned to lift Elyna into her arms. 'Hello, beautiful. You've grown so much.' Liza sank onto a chair still holding Elyna. 'I can't wait to chat about everything and hear how it's going with Etienne.'

The downside to catching up was Liza would want to know more than Camille was prepared to tell. Then again, what were best friends for if she couldn't download on Liza? Her chest felt full of liquid this morning. She couldn't believe how much she wanted Etienne's proposal to have been because he loved her and wanted to share his life with her. The realisation had dropped into her head with an almighty thud. It was true. She had fallen in love with him. Totally. If only he could do the same with her, but it was unlikely given his complete distrust of women.

She had her own trust issues, and they hadn't disappeared overnight, but more and more she was coming to think that if Etienne committed to someone—her—then he'd stay by her side for ever.

'Hello, Camille. Where have you gone?' Liza was watching her closely. 'I mention Etienne and you go blank on me.'

'Let's order coffee and breakfast before we talk about him. And your niece is wanting attention from Auntie Liza.'

Liza didn't stop looking at her for another long moment, then she kissed the top of Elyna's head. 'I've been longing to see you, sweetheart. You look pretty. Just like your mummy.'

'I'm not going to talk about Etienne no matter what you say.'

Liza was watching her closely. 'You look terrible, and since Elyna looks fine I can only think of one thing that could cause that. One person.'

It might be good to share her worries with her friend. 'I'm having croissants. You?'

'Same,' Liza said through a smile.

As the waitress placed plates of croissants on the table, Camille's phone pinged. An unknown number appeared on the screen. 'Hello?'

'Camille, it's Louise. I wanted to thank you for bringing Elyna to meet us yesterday. She's absolutely lovely and I hope we'll get to spend more time with her.' Etienne's mother sounded worried.

'Of course you will. You're her grandparents. I'd never get in the way of her being with you.'

'I'm sorry. I know that. You're so kind, but I'm prone to worrying about anything and everything. Ask Etienne.'

As if she was about to talk to him about his mother. She'd be lucky to hear from him at all today. That might be for the best with the state her mind was in. 'If you have any concerns call me and we'll talk about them.' As long as the family didn't want to take Elyna away from her and there'd been no suggestion of that so far.

'I should've said I rang Etienne for your number. I hope you don't mind. He sounded tired. Did you keep him up late?' Louise laughed.

'Um, no, I took Elyna home when she started getting scratchy.' She was allowed to tell little fibs, wasn't she? Better than telling Louise what she was struggling with. But it worried her that Louise might be thinking she was having another affair with her son. Not something she'd raise now, if at all. Etienne could sort that one out.

'You should've stayed and made Etienne take care of her, given yourself a break.'

He would've done that if necessary. But it hadn't been. 'I'll think about that next time.'

Coffee arrived.

'Thanks,' Camille said to the waitress.

'Sounds like you're busy. I'll let you go,' Louise said. 'Camille, please stay in touch and let me know what Elyna's up to.' Louise's wistfulness touched Camille. The woman wanted to be a part of her granddaughter's life and there was no way she'd prevent that. Elyna deserved to know all her family.

'I promise.' She hung up before the conversation continued and got deep.

'You've met Etienne's parents?' Liza asked with a sly smile. 'This gets more interesting by the day.'

'Yesterday. We had lunch with them at Etienne's.'

'So you've been to his house too. What's it like?'

Sometimes it didn't pay to tell her friend what was going on. Liza had no boundaries about what she asked or said. 'It's an old but well-cared-for mansion with lots of rooms and wonderful grounds. Stunning, really. It was stylish while keeping its history in the décor, and at the same time felt comfortable so that a person could do whatever they liked without ruining the atmosphere. A little girl could run around and not get in trouble for touching things.'

'So it's big enough for you and Elyna to live there and not be in Etienne's face all the time, then.'

As in not be married but in a family situation. No, thanks. It would play havoc with her heart. 'I suppose it is, but that's not happening. I've got my apartment, he's got his home, and we'll share raising Elyna accordingly.' She wouldn't mention the proposal to Liza, who'd pressure her to change her mind.

When Liza opened her mouth to say something

else, Camille raised her hand. 'No, Liza. Leave this to me to work my way through.'

'So you only want my shoulder to cry on when things go bad?' Liza sounded annoyed.

Now she'd gone and upset her friend. Getting up, she went around the table to hug her. 'I'm sorry. I do need you on my side. It's just that things are going well at the moment and I don't want to jeopardise it by overthinking or talking about what-ifs and maybes.' Not completely true, but best put that way for now.

'That's better.' Liza sniffed and grinned. 'It's all right. I think I understand. But don't let your past dictate how you unravel the future.'

Staring at her, Camille shook her head. 'Do you think that's what I'm doing? Letting my run of terrible men, including my birth father, get in the way of how I deal with Etienne?'

'Yes, I do. From the little you've told me he sounds like a decent guy who'd never let you or Elyna down.'

'He's a decent man, and he'll be a great dad, but I'm not living down the hallway from him.' It hadn't been suggested by Etienne but she felt it was coming as a second option to marriage. 'That would get in the way of me living my life how I want.' She'd love to live it with Etienne if he loved her, but that wasn't happening by the look of it. She certainly wasn't holding her breath, anyway.

* * *

Monday came around again and with it the first full week of her new job. Camille smiled as she walked onto the ward and looked around, excitement fizzing through her. She hadn't worked—not counting last week's few hours—since Elyna was born. She'd missed it. Nursing was in her blood. Caring for people came naturally and she always got a sense of withdrawal if she took too long away from it.

'Morning, Camille,' Karina called as she approached the nurses' station. 'Ready for a full-on week?'

'You bet.' Apart from dealing with Etienne's presence, she truly was. 'I've missed nursing.'

'We'll have you back up to speed before you know it. Take a seat and I'll run through some staff requisites that I should've done last week but didn't have time for.'

'That'll have to wait a while. I need one of you with George Spik. His abdominal wound has a serious infection.' Etienne stood in the doorway.

'Camille, can you take this one? I'm waiting for a call from Dr Elang in ED.'

'No problem.' Other than getting along as though nothing were wrong between them. Grabbing the thermometer, she followed Etienne, ignoring the thudding in her chest. 'Does the wound need redressing, or has it been done?'

Etienne spoke over his shoulder as he headed

down the ward. 'George pulled off the previous one. He's also pulled out his drip. He's running a fever and is very restless. I'm going to put in a new drip with increased antibiotics and analgesics, along with fluids.'

'When did you operate on him?'

'Friday afternoon. I dropped in first thing on Saturday on my way to pick you up and nothing was wrong then. According to the notes George started showing signs of infection late last night. Another specialist has been dealing with him, but I think the infection's getting worse.'

Etienne was treating her as he'd always done at work. One less thing to worry about. But then she'd have been surprised if he'd been aloof around here. Too many people would notice and question it. 'Are you taking him back to Theatre?'

'Most likely. I did bowel surgery for cancer on him but a major infection is unusual.' The worry in his voice caught at Camille.

'Don't start blaming yourself. It might be unusual, but it does happen.'

He stopped and stared at her for a long moment. Then he dipped his head and carried on as though nothing had happened.

But it had. A flicker of gratitude had flashed across his face. Didn't he expect her to say what she believed because of what had happened between them? If so, he didn't know her very well, which he didn't, really. She'd thought she was getting to know Etienne, but she never would have seen his proposal coming. Or his shock when she turned him down.

Following Etienne into the room and across to his patient, she focused entirely on George and what Etienne wanted her to do. 'You want a new dressing, obs and a sponge down.' The man was bathed in sweat.

'Yes.' He leaned down. 'George, can you hear me?'

George opened his eyes. 'Doctor.'

'Good. George, this is Nurse Camille. She's going to be looking after you. I've looked at the wound, and we need to go back into Theatre.'

'Why?'

'I need to find out why you've got an infection.'

'Did you have breakfast, George?' Camille asked. Fingers crossed he hadn't.

'No. Too sick.'

'That's a plus,' Etienne said. 'I don't want to hang about on this.'

Camille placed the thermometer in George's ear. 'Thirty nine point nine.'

Etienne nodded, unsurprised. 'Keep a running tally and let me know if it goes up at all.'

'Absolutely. I'll get the gear to put a dressing on in the meantime.' Plus cloths to give George a good wipe down.

'I'll stay with him until you return,' Etienne told her.

She headed quickly for the storeroom where everything used for patient care was kept. Etienne was in doctor mode, not a hint of how he felt about her showing on his face. Hopefully she appeared just as calm. Though she wasn't known for being able to hide her feelings very well so chances were he knew how wound up she was.

Returning to George, she drank in the sight of the gorgeous man standing at the bedside who was doing her head in. If only he didn't have hang-ups about laying his heart on the line. But even if he didn't that didn't mean he'd fall for her. She wasn't his type. What was his type? Confident, poised, used to a very different lifestyle from hers. Not forgetting he was kind, gentle and caring, and not only with patients. He'd been marvellous with Elyna and the same with his parents. Be honest, he was like that with her too. Ka-thump went her heart.

'I've arranged time in Theatre at midday,' Etienne informed her.

'You want me at his side until then, don't you?'

'Yes, I do. Call me if anything changes. Even if it's only point one on his temperature reading.'

'I will.'

He turned to head away, then hesitated and came back to her. 'Thank you, Camille.'

What for? She was only doing her job.

'For not making this any more difficult than it already is.' Then he was gone.

Leaving her stunned yet again. He really could surprise her with his openness at times. 'George, I'm going to clean the wound and then put a new dressing on to protect it until Dr Laval sees you in Theatre.' Etienne intrigued her. A lot. Was there a possibility he might want to get closer to her? To become more than joint parents? It didn't seem likely considering their very different backgrounds, but, as Grandma would've said, anything was possible given half a chance.

'Whatever,' the man on the bed croaked.

Lifting the bedcover away from George's midriff, she began cleaning the red, swollen septic area with antibiotic fluid, careful not to press too hard and cause more distress. Next she placed a wide dressing over the area, keeping the tape away from the wound. 'I'm going to give you a good wipe down all over, and make you feel a little more comfortable.'

'I c-can't stop s-sweating.'

'The infection's doing that. Have you had any rigors? Severe shaking,' she added in case he didn't know what she meant.

'Once. I told D-Dr L-Laval.'

'Good. Remember to tell me if there's anything else that feels abnormal. The more we know, the easier it is for Dr Laval to get on top of the infection and its consequences.'

'He said the s-same.'

'Do you feel hot or cold?'

'Both at d-different times. Cold now.'

Hence his stutter. 'I'll get another cover for you once I've finished cleaning you up.'

On her way to the linen room for the cover she stopped at the desk to call Etienne. 'George is having more rigors. I'm about to put another bedcover over him. He's stuttering quite a bit.'

'What about his temperature?'

'That's remained the same as when you were up here.' It hadn't been very long since she'd taken the temperature with Etienne watching but it was something she'd keep doing regularly until he said to stop.

'Arrange for an orderly to bring him down to Theatre three in thirty minutes. There's been a cancellation and I've grabbed the spot.' The line went dead.

'On it,' Camille said into the air. He was getting on with his job, and she with hers despite the image of his handsome face loitering in the back of her head to be looked at whenever she had a moment to spare. He was something else. A man of his word. To be trusted? She believed so, but that didn't mean she was ready to risk taking a chance. Anyway, she'd already turned down his offer of marriage and there was no other relationship she wanted long term.

Two hours later George was brought back up to the ward and Camille returned to his bed to check his obs after reading the notes to see what Etienne had found when he'd gone into the infected site. Three internal sutures had been pulled free so that blood had leaked into the bowel, and infection had set in.

'He must've jerked hard or tripped badly to have caused that,' Etienne said over her shoulder. 'He says he slipped in the shower the morning after I operated but that it was nothing serious. I wonder if he downplayed it because he'd ignored the nurse who'd told him to remain in bed until she was available to oversee his shower.'

'Very likely. It's not the first time I've known a patient to do that. Especially men when their nurse is female.'

'What time are you knocking off?' Etienne asked.

'I've got nearly an hour to go.' Working alongside Etienne had always made her feel good. He appreciated the nurses and never acted superior. More than that, he was happy to discuss cases as though nurses understood everything he talked about. Nothing had changed despite the elephant looming between them.

'Can I call in later to see Elyna?'

'Of course you can. I'm not going anywhere.' Sounded pathetic, but she could justify it because Elyna would be tired after spending half the day in the crèche. 'Maybe you could take her for a walk in the park if she's up to it.'

'I won't be away from here before dark.'

Of course he wouldn't. 'I need to put my thinking cap on. I'll take her for a walk. Might go past the Eiffel Tower. I'm catching up with my city and hoping to instill in Elyna a sense of where she belongs.'

'How about I bring dinner with me?'

She thought he was coming to see Elyna, not her. Did she want him staying past Elyna's bedtime? She had no idea what she wanted. There was only one way to find out. 'That'd be great.'

'Anything you don't eat?'

'Not really. Just don't go overboard with something whacky.' She dredged up a smile to show she wasn't being too serious.

'I'll behave.' His grin looked more honest than her smile felt, plus it was reassuring, which surprised her. He was trying to move on while she kept going over and over his proposal and all it meant.

'Good.' In some ways he was a different man from the lover she'd known. He'd been kind and fun then, not deep and personal. Though personal was still a fair way off, when she thought about it. Which she did far too much.

'See you later.' He hadn't looked around to make sure no one was within hearing. Was he prepared to let others know there was more to them than a doctor-nurse relationship?

She shrugged the idea away. It was ridiculous

when he'd always been very careful about what people knew about his private life. 'Okay.' She started checking George's obs. Work would keep the mind busy and errant thoughts about Etienne at bay. Or so she hoped.

CHAPTER SEVEN

'ELYNA, DADDY'S HERE.' Etienne swooped his girl up with his free arm and lightly kissed her scrunched-up face. His heart expanded with love, such a new emotion for him, and showed him he really, truly did accept she was his daughter. Glancing around, he found Camille staring at him with wonder in those beautiful eyes, from which a stray tear fell. 'Yes, I'm Daddy.' Stepping across the gap between them, he brushed a kiss over Camille's lips. 'Thank you for sharing her with me. Imagine if you'd never told me? But then I suppose I'd never have known what I was missing out on.'

She blanched. 'Elyna deserves better than that. So do we.'

'I know. I might not know you as well as I'd like to yet, but I know that you are a straight shooter when it comes to the truth.'

She shook her head as if she didn't quite know where to go from here.

He had a few ideas but had learned to go cautiously. 'Elyna's my daughter.' It was the absolute truth.

Tears poured out of Camille's eyes. 'Th-that is th-the b-best thing you could ever have said.'

Putting down the bag he was carrying, he put his free arm around her shoulders and tucked her in against him. He liked making Camille happy. It made him feel happy right down to his toes and back again. With Camille in one arm, Elyna in the other, it couldn't get much better than this. Nodding at the bag, he said, 'I've brought wine from home. Let's have a toast to parenthood.'

Pulling away, Camille said, 'I seem to always be drinking wine, but yes, let's celebrate. I've waited a long time for this.'

'I've ordered chicken fricassee from the restaurant along the road to be delivered at seven-thirty. I've been assured they know what they're doing.'

Finally a small smile lightened her face. 'Five stars do kind of indicate that.' She took the bag and headed to the kitchen, saying over her shoulder, 'It's lovely of you to do this.'

'Any time.' Strange, but he meant it. He'd be happy to turn up every night with a meal to share with her along with wine and light-hearted chatter about their day.

Elyna wriggled in his arm, obviously impatient for some attention. 'Yes, I've got something for you too.' He dug into his jacket pocket and tugged out a small woollen toy. 'Here you go, little one. It's a dog.' He held it out to her. 'Can you say dog?'

Elyna grabbed the toy, a large smile on her face.

'Say dog, Elyna.' Camille was back, watching her daughter as she stared at her gift.

'Og.' Elyna kissed it. 'Mama, og.'

'Say thanks to Daddy.'

Elyna cuddled the soft toy close and stared at him.

'Any time.' He placed her carefully on the floor. 'There you go.' Looking at Camille, he could feel his heart expanding further. They really were a family. A disjointed one for now, yes, but making inroads into sorting it out. If Camille had accepted his proposal they'd be further on with doing that, but he hadn't given up. Next time he asked her to marry him it would be with all his heart, or not at all.

'I've talked to your mother twice since we saw her on Saturday. She'd like to have Elyna for the day on Friday. It'll be good for Elyna to get to know her plus not to have to be at the crèche every day of the week.'

'Mum's going to ask to have her one day every week.' His mother was giddy with excitement over her granddaughter.

'That'd be wonderful. I do feel bad about leaving her in the crèche so often.'

'Do you work because you need the income or

because you enjoy nursing so much?' He had no idea how Camille was situated financially, and it wasn't an easy discussion to have when she was so fiercely independent.

'Both.' Sinking onto the arm of a lounge chair, she looked up at him. 'I'm fortunate to be able to support us as long as I'm careful. It was a toss-up about whether to get a job or not, but in the end I do need to add to my savings and also being a solo parent is hard enough without having some time with other people every day. In Montreal I spent all my time caring for Grandma and looking after Elyna so became a little lonely.' She paused, her fingers flexing on her thighs. 'I also think it's good for Elyna to be with other children.'

'Camille, I'm not going to criticise your decisions. I'm sure it's not easy doing this on your own. I'm here to help and be a part of her life no matter what.' He'd never dodge his responsibilities. It wasn't in his DNA. 'I'd like to set up a bank account for her, under your name, of course.'

'That's not necessary.'

'But it is part of being her father. I'm not undermining what you do, Camille, merely contributing to her financial needs going forward.'

Silence.

Finally Camille nodded abruptly. 'Fair enough.'

She could sound more enthusiastic, but this

was Camille. Her strength beguiled him. Add in her sexiness and he was a goner long before he'd realised how much he'd missed her when she'd walked away. 'We'll talk more about it later.' He wasn't changing his mind, just giving her time to fully accept his offer.

She stood up and rubbed her lower back, drawing his eyes there and then lower to her curvy bottom. 'I'll get the wine.'

Definitely sexy. Which added to the things that needed sorting out between them because spending as much time with her as he intended so he'd see enough of Elyna was going to keep him continuously hard and aching with need. Need for Camille. Not a need that could be met by any other woman. 'I'd like a glass of Merlot. It's one of the best from the family winery. My brother-in-law's a great winemaker.'

A laugh escaped those tempting lips as she unscrewed the bottle. 'I'm no expert when it comes to wine but I know what I like and where some of it comes from.'

'Would you like to visit the family vineyards some time?'

Her head shot up, her eyes wide with enthusiasm. 'I'd love to. I've never been on a vineyard. Haven't spent a lot of time out of cities at all.'

Happiness at offering Camille something that seemed to delight her glowed in his chest. All was going well. Careful, don't spoil things by tempting fate. They still had a lot to work through. 'I'll arrange a trip soon. You need to meet my sister and her husband and my nephews.'

'I presume they've heard about Elyna.'

'You don't think my mum or dad could keep quiet about her, do you? Anyway, I've talked to Cariole so she knows what's going on.'

Worry filtered through Camille's eyes. 'How did she take it?'

'She's thrilled. She's always nagging me to find a woman and settle down to raise a brood. Hopefully she'll shut up now.' Not until he was married, but best to keep that to himself.

'That's a relief. My biggest fear, after telling you, was what the rest of your family would say. I came up with a hundred scenarios and most of them weren't good.'

He couldn't help himself. He stepped close to wrap his arms around her, pulling her against his chest. And breathed in her floral scent. 'You worry too much.'

'Hard not to when I knew I was tossing a hand grenade into your life.' Tension rippled through her, making him realise again how difficult all this had been for her.

'We're surviving.'

Camille moved away to finish pouring the wine and handed him a glass. 'Take a seat and relax. Watch Elyna playing with her new toy and enjoy your time with her. She'll be going to bed soon.'

He wanted to say Elyna could stay up a bit later tonight, but he wasn't the one who'd have to put up with a cranky child in the morning. Besides, Camille was right not to change their routine for him. He was the one who had to fit in with them. 'Hey, Elyna, what are you going to call the dog?'

'Og.' She beamed at him as she hugged the small toy to her chest. 'Og!'

'Guess that's going to stick.' Camille chuckled as she sat opposite him. 'Until her speech improves anyway.'

At least she liked the toy, he thought. He hadn't had a clue what to buy when he'd decided to bring her a present. There didn't appear to be a lot of toys around the apartment, but that could be because Camille's possessions were still en route by sea. 'When do your boxes arrive from Montreal?'

She swung Elyna up into her arms. 'Hopefully at the end of next week. Both of us could do with some more clothes now we've settled in and I'm working.'

About to offer to take her shopping, he stopped. That was wrong in all aspects. Camille would turn him down but the fact he'd thought to offer at all was a total turnaround on protecting his heart. But then he was already losing ground there. And enjoying it. More than he'd ever have believed. 'Is it bedtime for Elyna?'

'Story time and then fingers crossed she'll fall asleep.' Camille sent him a cheeky smile. 'You up to reading about turtles?'

'I can hardly wait.' He used to read to his nephews at bedtime but this was different. Elyna was *his daughter*. So yes, he truly couldn't wait.

Within minutes Elyna was tucked up in bed, the cuddly toy held tight against her tiny chest and her eyes filled with expectation. 'Story.'

Sitting on the edge of the bed, Etienne opened the large book filled with pictures that Camille had handed him and began reading the story, altering his voice for each character and making Elyna laugh. Which was so wonderful he became almost tearful. Sucking in his chest, he toughened up and got on with entertaining Elyna.

If only it were as easy to captivate her mother.

After watching Elyna grinning as her father read to her last night, Camille knew her relationship with Etienne had changed for ever. It didn't matter what lay ahead, he was smitten and would be a big part of Elyna's life. Where that left *her* was anyone's guess. Only time would tell, unless she confronted Etienne to start making some decisions about caring for their daughter. It was complicated with both of them working and therefore not always there for her. Living in different areas of the city didn't help either.

Despite everything she didn't regret turning down his proposal. She believed in love, and not even for her daughter was she going into a one-sided marriage. Etienne might have captured her heart, but if he didn't return those feelings then she couldn't bear the thought of sharing his house, and no doubt the marital bed. Oh, she wanted sex with him. Absolutely. The memories of their previous times together remained with her for a reason—he was incredibly hot. And his lovemaking skills were beyond belief. But she was not getting married for great sex alone. What if another woman came into his life who he fell in love with? Where would that leave Elyna? It would break *her* heart, but what would it do to his daughter's?

'Morning, Camille.' The man raising these questions stood at the nurses' station.

Her stomach rolled as her eyes roamed over his sensational body dressed in a perfectly fitted grey suit and white shirt, looking good enough to eat despite her concerns. How had she ever managed to turn him down? 'Morning, Etienne. I see we're getting two of your patients from Theatre later.' Keep everything focused on work, not sexy bodies. Body. Etienne's was the only one she was interested in.

His smile dimmed a little. 'Yes. Carlos Bruffin has a serious prostate infection that hasn't improved since he was admitted thirty-six hours ago for fluids and antibiotics. I'm going to open him up and see what's causing the problem. There's a lump that may be the reason.'

She winced. 'The poor man.'

'Agreed. He's not happy about the procedure but it's that or the infection could turn to septicaemia.' Etienne shrugged those wide shoulders. 'I don't have any alternative.'

He'd hate it but he also wouldn't hesitate if it meant saving the man's life. 'No, you don't. I read Mrs Gossim's file.' The thirty-five-year-old woman had had breast cancer five years ago, and was now dealing with multiple tumours in her bowel. Camille shuddered. Horrific to be facing that at any age, but she was far too young.

Etienne's face turned grim. 'It's not looking good, but if anything's on Sophie's side, it's that she's very positive and upbeat.'

'I've worked with patients like that, and the bad days when they run out of steam are dreadful.'

Looking steadily at her, Etienne nodded. 'You're so understanding. No wonder I like working with you.'

The steel protecting her heart softened. He got to her far too easily. Face it, she liked that he saw behind her determination to be strong and not depend on anyone else to get through life's battles. He'd made her think she could let go of her past hurts and move forward to a place where she felt safe to give her heart away completely. 'Thank you,' she whispered.

A phone rang.

Etienne pulled his from his pocket. 'Hello?' He watched her while listening to whoever was on the other end of the call. 'I'm on my way.' He slid the phone back in his pocket. 'A patient in emergency needs urgent abdominal surgery after falling onto a metal stake in the garden. I'll see you later if you're still on duty when my other patients are brought up.'

Chances were slight as she had less than three hours to go and he'd likely be tied up for all that. Warring with the disappointment that had no right to raise its head here at work, she nodded. 'Sure.'

His long legs ate up the distance to the elevators, filling her with a longing that had no place in her heart. Except it was already there. What a man. She sighed and picked up the hospital phone to find out if the emergency patient Etienne was about to operate on would be coming up to this ward.

The woman certainly knew how to tip him sideways, Etienne admitted as he rode the elevator down three floors to Theatre. What was worse was that she didn't even try to get him onside.

Probably why knocking him off balance worked so easily.

Camille would laugh her head off if she knew how much sleep he'd missed out on since she'd come back into his life. Every time he put his head on the pillow and closed his eyes there she was: smiling, growling, talking, attending to a patient, cuddling Elyna. Looking soft and kind, hot and sexy, angry and determined. Then he'd get up in the morning and go to work only to bump into the real-life version—which wasn't any different from the one in his mind. There was no getting away from her.

He needed to grin and bear it. They were always going to be a part of each other's lives because of Elyna. If she agreed to his next suggestion he'd be seeing even more of her. Yes, he had another idea to put to her.

His phone rang. The head of the surgical department's name appeared on the screen. A timely reminder to get back to thinking about patients and not Camille. 'Louis, what's up?'

'I need you on call for the rest of the week. Jason has had to take time off to go to Tours. His son's been in a serious accident and it's not known if he'll make it through surgery.'

His stomach tightened. The poor guy. No parent would ever want to go through that. Of course, now he was a parent himself it had become a lot more real to think that. 'Of course I'll take over. No problem.'

'Thanks, Etienne. Knew you wouldn't mind stepping up. I'll see you in Theatre shortly.' Louis was gone, no doubt busy sorting the roster before going in to operate on someone.

'Guess I won't be spending much time with Camille and Elyna this week.' Etienne sighed as the door slid open and he stepped out onto his floor. That might be a good thing, giving him more time to think about Camille turning down his proposal and try to see it from her point of view so he got it right with his next idea. She might also understand his suggestion and see he wasn't always going to be available to drop by her place to spend time with his daughter. Yes, this could actually play into his hands.

It sounded as though he was scheming to have his own way. Guess he was a little, but wasn't it also in Camille and Elyna's best interests to live with him? Or near him, at least?

Later that night when he'd finished up in Theatre after an appendectomy on a young boy, he called Camille. 'Hi, I'd hoped to get to see Elyna tonight but I've been rostered on call and have just finished an urgent surgery.'

'It can't be helped. She's already tucked up in bed sound asleep.'

'I figured she would be.' It was well after her bedtime. 'I'll try again tomorrow night.'

'There's always the spare room here if at any time you don't want to go all the way to your place.'

Seriously? Did Camille just offer him a bed? A solo one, of course. Which would make sleep impossible with her only a door away. 'Thanks. I might take you up on that some time, but not tonight. I haven't got spare clothes with me.' When he knew he was on call he usually stayed in the doctors' quarters to save himself the tedious drive from his house, and now he had another option. He'd have to think about that. It could be great spending even more time with Camille in her home, but it might also add to his concerns over getting too close to her. What if she found a man she loved and moved in with him? They wouldn't be sharing homes then. Life would become tricky when it came to visiting Elyna. He wanted to slam the phone down and head to her place right this minute to make her see they had to work something out to everyone's benefit.

'I'll see you on the ward tomorrow.' She didn't sound too disappointed that he wasn't about to turn up at her apartment, but he'd have been more surprised if she was.

'Goodnight, Camille.' He hung up before he could change his mind and make an idiot of himself.

***

Friday night and Etienne was at Camille's for dinner after another busy day. Since the roster changed on Fridays he was no longer on call so there was no chance of being called away before he got down to business. She'd suggested he come to see Elyna and stay for a meal so they could have some time together. He wasn't quite sure what time together meant but was more than willing to go along with it as he'd already intended dropping in to put forward his suggestion regarding where she might like to live.

'Would you like more casserole?' Camille asked.

'That was delicious but I couldn't eat another mouthful. You certainly know how to cook.' It had been a simple but tasty meal he'd eat any day of the week.

'Cooking is my go to when I want to clear my head of other things.' She actually blushed. A rare sight. The dark pink hue suited her. 'I have a lot of great memories of spending time in the kitchen with Grandma.'

'There's always so much affection in your voice when you talk of your grandparents. They were good to you, weren't they?'

'Absolutely. They gave up their dream of travelling the world when I was born. Then when I was old enough to get on with my life and they could go away for long periods, Grandpa was too sick, but not once did I feel I was to blame for them missing out on their dream. I couldn't have been luckier having them raise me.' She paused, looked around the dining room, then continued. 'Naturally I always wondered what my life might've been like if my mother had lived and brought me up, and what I might've missed out on. But in the end, there's nothing I could've changed, and I'm not sure I'd want to.'

'Pragmatic, aren't you?'

'Too much time can be wasted trying to alter the unchangeable. I wasted a lot as a kid wishing for my mother not to be dead and for my father to come get me. Then when he did turn up I knew I'd been lucky without him in my day-to-day life.'

'You make me even more grateful for my family. They've been my rocks.' Always there when he needed support, to celebrate when he achieved a goal, to love him without qualification. 'Like your grandparents, I suppose.'

'Yes, and how I intend being for Elyna.'

His heart swelled yet again. 'Me, too.' Time to put it out there. 'Which is why I'd like to suggest you both move into my house. That way we can share looking after Elyna more easily.'

Camille turned thoughtful, giving him no clue to what she was thinking. 'Do you think that'd work? Sharing a house when we're not in a relationship?'

'As you've seen, it's not a small place. You'd

have your own rooms. We'd have to share the kitchen, although your cooking is so good I'm happy to leave the kitchen to you,' he said in an attempt to lighten her mood.

She flicked him a half-hearted smile. 'Knew I shouldn't have made dinner again. Seriously, I understand where you're coming from.'

Here comes the 'but'. He still wasn't used to hearing it. It stung. He was trying to do what was right by all of them and yet Camille was persistent in turning him down.

'I've only just got back home and I need time here to feel properly settled. I got such a bang on the heart when I walked in here the day I returned and I don't know that I'm ready to move away from this apartment quite yet.'

A picture of those tears streaking down her face crossed his mind, tapping his own heart. 'I understand. You want more time. That's fine.' He could be patient. But they did have to make some serious decisions about how they lived so they could raise Elyna between them. On the other hand, time might help him overcome the need to be with her more often. 'I don't want you regretting a decision further down the track.' There was no avoiding his disappointment though. It would be awesome having Camille in his home, and Elyna racing around in her crazy little girl way.

Camille locked those lovely eyes on him and this time her smile was soft. 'None of this is easy for you, I know that. I've had longer to get used to being a parent, and to think about how to sort out the future. You're just getting started.'

'It's been quite a ride so far but I don't regret any of it.'

One eyebrow rose. 'Truly?'

'Truly.' Enough. Next he'd be admitting how he'd tried to find her after she'd left Paris. Now was not the time for that. The right moment might never arrive. Standing up, he took their plates to the sink to rinse them off before placing them in the dishwasher. 'I'll look in on Elyna, then I'd better head home. The week's catching up with me. I got called in every night.'

'That's rough. I admit to feeling tired after going to work every day this week. I'm out of practice and they're only short shifts.'

'Mum said you looked a little worn out when you collected Elyna earlier.'

Camille nodded. 'From the way she was hugging Louise when I got there to pick her up, Elyna had a great time. I doubt there'll be any problems with her going there regularly.'

'Good. That makes everyone happy.' Another box ticked. This was going well except when it came to the big issues, like his proposal and where Camille and Elyna should live.

Camille said, 'We'll see you over the weekend.'

It wasn't a question. She knew he'd be here at some point. Unless… 'How about we go to the vineyard tomorrow? You can meet the rest of the family. Pack an overnight bag and we'll stay the night.' His mouth had got away on him. Didn't he realise he was not looking to fall in love with Camille? Except he suspected he was already partway there.

She hesitated, then gulped. 'All right. I'll say yes to tomorrow and see how Elyna goes before agreeing to stay longer.'

'Fair enough.' Was she using Elyna to get out of spending too long with his family?

'If she throws a tantrum I won't use that as an excuse to leave, I promise,' she added.

'And if you throw one?' he asked with a forced laugh.

'Then your family will be lining up to toss me out.' Her return smile loosened the knots that had risen in his gut. 'I know this is all part of getting to know each other. I get nervous, that's all.'

'You've already won over my parents so I doubt there'll be any problems with the rest of the tribe.' Time to say goodnight to his daughter and get out of here before he said anything he might regret.

Elyna looked so sweet tucked under her bedcover with Og clutched in her arms that he actually had to brush a tear away before returning to the kitchen to say bye to Camille.

Except she was standing in the bedroom doorway watching him as he made to leave the room and his heart clenched. 'Camille,' he whispered around the lump in his throat.

She reached over to wipe a second tear from his cheek with her finger. 'It's all going to work out, I promise.'

He didn't realise his arms were going around her, pulling her in close. He couldn't have said how long he gazed into those mesmerising eyes before he lowered his head to kiss her full lips. Not a light brush over them but his mouth covering hers, feeling their warmth and fullness. His tongue slipped inside her mouth and tasted her. His arms tightened their hold on the gorgeous body pressed up against his.

Her mouth opened under his, accepting him further. Her hands cradled his head as she pressed against him.

'Oh, Camille,' he whispered.

She jerked her head back, staring at him in consternation before stepping out of his arms. 'This has to stop now,' she muttered.

She was right, it did. But for the life of him he did not want to walk away from her. He wanted her. He was hard for her. He spun around and headed for the main door. 'Goodnight.'

She didn't answer.

Camille's fingers traced her lips. Etienne had kissed her again. She'd bet her pay packet he hadn't intended to. He'd looked surprised when she'd pulled back. She'd been surprised when he'd leaned into the kiss that had turned her on so fast she was still trying to quieten her body. The kiss that took all reason from her mind. Thankfully she'd come to her senses before they'd gone too far.

Tell that to your body.

She was trying. Gazing down at her daughter, she swallowed the need clawing at her. 'Your father's the most wonderful man I've ever known.' She had to remain strong in the face of his attractiveness. They were not becoming a couple when he didn't love her. She was still coming to terms with the fact that she loved Etienne. She could admit it to herself anyway. She didn't need to mess things up by agreeing to marry him. What about moving into his house? That would be no easier when every time she saw him he took her breath away.

Living together was a good idea as far as Elyna was concerned, but not so much for her. She and Etienne would be forever bumping into each other. Different from working together where there were staff and patients to keep their feet on the ground. In the house there'd be no getting away from him for long periods, and that would not help with getting over him. If that was even possible now.

She'd got over Benoit fairly quickly because he'd been so dishonest about his marriage and family that her heart had rejected him, leaving her with a weight of distrust when it came to loving again. Etienne wouldn't lie to her, wouldn't go behind her back, but she still wasn't prepared to be at his side when he didn't love her.

CHAPTER EIGHT

'The weather's diabolical at the vineyards,' Etienne told Camille over the phone the next morning. 'I think it's better if we give going up there a miss. I don't want the weather interfering with driving home again as I'm flying down to Nice first thing Monday morning for a two-day get-together with other specialists.'

First she'd heard of it but they didn't share everything. Camille looked out of the lounge window as a gust of wind rattled the glass. 'The rain's not far off here either.' Over the road at the hotel tourists were dressed in jackets and boots. This was why most people visited the city in summer, she thought, shaking her head.

'How about you come here for the day? There's plenty of room for Elyna to charge around and you can have another look around the house in case you do decide to live here.'

His offer wasn't going away. It would hang between them like a wrecking ball, though, to be fair, at the moment it was still only a suggestion.

Could she spend the day in his house without getting too uptight about the decision she had to make? He understood she wasn't ready to leave her own home. The time away in Montreal had been too long and not getting back to life as she used to know and like it had affected her. She'd never have insisted her grandmother return to Paris when she became so ill, and she'd never regret staying to look after her, but now that she was back she was soaking up her history and starting to get into the life of motherhood as she'd believed it should be. Etienne was wanting to change everything too soon.

'Hello? Are you still there?' He cut through her thoughts, his deep voice reminding her of his lips on hers, his tongue exploring her mouth. So much for forgetting the kiss. She could feel his hands on her waist, his chest against her breasts. And he was only talking to her—over the darned phone, at that!

'Yes. We'll come out to your house,' she snapped in an effort to put that kiss behind her. 'I'll take the train, save you coming here.'

'No, Camille. I have to get a few things at the supermarket and can do that on the way, unless you need anything.'

She wasn't going to win about the train, and as she did need some food items for Elyna she might as well go with his offer. It would keep her onside. Something that was necessary if this was going to be a pleasant weekend not filled with disagreements and constantly being on edge. 'Actually, I do. All right, I'll get organised so we're ready when you get here.' The large last-century clock on the lounge wall had barely ticked past eight, but she doubted he'd take all morning to turn up.

'That should be some time after ten. I'll go to the market first to get fresh fruit and vegetables, and some cheeses.'

Her mouth watered. Nothing like a good cheese for a snack. 'See you later.' She hung up before he heard her stomach growling at the thought of cheese. Her favourite food, along with chicken, beef, vegetables, everything.

Smacking her forehead lightly, she grinned. She felt good, very good, despite spending the day with Etienne. Or because of that? Most likely. 'Elyna, we're going to Daddy's for the day.' Maybe longer. She'd pack enough gear for two days, just in case.

Her phone rang again. Etienne. 'Did you forget you had to be in London for the weekend?' she laughed.

'Pack something to wear in case we go out for dinner.' He hung up.

As if they'd go out when Elyna was there. Unless Louise and Hugo were going to be there too? Surely he'd have told her if that was so? He didn't hide things like that from her. He was more inclined to keep her up-to-date so that she couldn't say he was being sneaky.

Standing in front of her sparse wardrobe, she shook her head in dismay. The clothes hanging there were more than two years old and had fitted her well before Elyna came along. Her curves were a little more accentuated these days. The outfits she'd bought since then were somewhere at sea in a container along with everything else she'd collected while in Montreal. Glancing hopefully at the time, she groaned in despair. There wasn't time to catch a train to the nearest clothing outlet and get back before Etienne arrived. Was there?

'Elyna, come on, we're going out.'

By the time they returned to her apartment with two bags of clothes she was in a panic. She still had to pack clothes and toys for Elyna, plus other essentials, and Etienne's car was parked on the other side of the road.

He got out as she reached the main entrance to the apartment building.

'You're early,' she puffed before he could comment on her being late.

'I must be on a different timeframe from you.' He grinned as he took the pram from her. 'Hello, little one. I see Mummy's been shopping.'

Of course, it was obvious by the logos on the bags she carried where she'd been. Then he eyeballed her. 'You didn't have to go shopping for something to wear tonight.'

Oh, yes, she did. She wasn't going out with Etienne looking like something dragged out of the recycle bin. This was the man of her dreams and even if he was only taking her out to be friendly she wasn't going to look a mess. 'I'm short on decent clothes at the moment.' There wasn't that much extra clothing coming from Canada. She'd been careful with her money over there, not wanting to delve too often into her bank accounts where her inheritance was invested.

'Then I'd better make sure my parents do come to babysit. I'd hate for you to have wasted your morning shopping.' He was grinning so hard her head spun.

She'd never seen Etienne like this before. She liked it. It was as though he was ready to show her more of who he really was. 'No such thing as wasting time when it comes to shopping. Not that I do a lot of it.'

He was still grinning as he retorted, 'You're a female. You expect me to believe that?'

'Naturally.'

'Let's get upstairs so you can pack whatever Elyna needs and then we'll hit the road.' He swung the pram towards the entrance and keyed in the code number she'd given him at the outset.

'I won't be long.' Yeah, right. She hadn't packed a thing before rushing out to go to the shops.

'Don't panic. We've got all day.' He was still grinning. Whatever he'd had for breakfast she wanted some. It made him relaxed and happy.

Etienne wished he could take those words back after he heard someone pounding on Camille's door and a woman calling out, 'Camille, are you there? I need you.'

Camille was in Elyna's bedroom putting a bag of things together.

'There's someone at your door. It sounds urgent,' he told her. 'Want me to see what's up?'

'I'm coming with you.' She brushed past him as she strode to the door. Pulling it open, she said quietly, 'Hello, Maree. What's up?'

'It's Jules. He's fallen and can't speak. I don't know what's going on.'

'We'll come and see him. Maree, this is a friend, Etienne. He's a doctor. You take him to Jules while I put Elyna in her pram with some toys. We'll join you in a moment.'

So, he was only a friend? I'm more than that, Camille, he thought to himself as he followed the distressed woman down to the next apartment. 'Maree, did Jules complain about pain, or a headache before he fell?'

'Earlier he said his head felt funny, but then he seemed to come right.'

A stroke perhaps. 'Has he a history of headaches or feeling funny?'

'*Non.* He's always been healthy. I'm the one who gets sick. In here.'

He followed Maree inside the apartment, thinking how often stroke sufferers had been healthy beforehand. On the floor in the hallway lay a large man, sprawled awkwardly. 'You haven't tried to move him at all?'

'No, I ran to get Camille. I didn't want to make anything worse for Jules.'

'So you haven't called an ambulance?' Etienne asked as he knelt down beside Jules and felt for a pulse. It was there, weak but steady.

'Should I?'

'Jules, can you hear me?'

One eye opened slowly.

Etienne nodded. 'That's a yes. Maree, call SAMU now.' He didn't want to frighten the woman any further, but an ambulance was required urgently. 'When you get through hand me the phone so I can explain what's going on.' Pressing his fingers on Jules' arms, then abdomen, legs, and getting no reaction confirmed his suspicions.

Camille knelt down on the opposite side of the man. 'What have we got?'

He glanced around to see where Maree was, and, not seeing her, nodded to Camille. 'I think he's had a stroke.'

'Jules, it's Camille.' She was taking his pulse as she talked. 'I'm sorry I haven't had time to catch up with you since returning home. You haven't met my daughter either. Maree did when we shared the elevator the other day.' She carried on chatting quietly as though nothing were wrong. 'Pulse normal but unsteady,' she said in an aside to him.

'We need to roll him onto his side.'

'No problem.' Together they straightened Jules enough to get him onto his side and his head tipped back a little to ease his breathing.

Maree approached, worry filling her face. 'They want to talk to you.' She handed him her phone. 'The ambulance is coming.'

He stood up and walked a few steps away. 'This is Etienne Laval, a general surgeon at Central Hospital. I believe the man's had a stroke.'

'A serious one?'

'Yes. He does respond to questions by lifting one eyelid very slowly. Other than that, there's no reaction to touches or moving his limbs.'

'I'll inform the paramedic heading your way.'

He pressed off and returned to Jules, where Camille was taking a blanket from Maree and tucking it around the man. 'Can you get a pillow?' he asked.

Maree rushed away.

'On their way?' Camille asked him.

'Yes. I wonder if Maree might go down to let them in when they arrive?'

'I want to stay with Jules,' Maree said as she handed Camille the pillow.

'Of course you do. Will you go in the ambulance with him?'

'Yes.'

'You'll need to take your phone and card with you,' he told Maree, watching Camille ever so gently place the pillow under her neighbour's neck. 'Where's Elyna?' he asked.

'Buckled in her pram in Maree's dining room with Og and a teddy to keep her entertained. Unless she drops them.'

'I reckon we'd hear her if that happened.' His little girl was not known for being quiet when something went wrong.

Camille flicked him a smile that went straight to his gut. 'True.'

One smile and he was thinking of Camille naked in his arms as they made love. It was sex. No, lovemaking. Whichever, he just remembered those nights far too graphically.

'If you like I'll go down and wait for the ambulance. I'll take Elyna with me. She's bundled up warm.'

That'd give him breathing space. Which he didn't really want, but it would be quicker if one of them was there to meet the medics. 'All right. Hopefully you won't have to wait long.'

'Jules, I'm going downstairs to wait for the ambulance. Etienne will stay with you and make sure you're all right until the medics arrive.' Camille stood up, and looked at him. Sadness filled her face. 'I've known him most of my life,' she said quietly.

Stepping around Jules, he wrapped his arms gently around her for a moment. 'Deep breaths.' He wasn't going to say something like Jules would be all right because they had no idea what lay ahead and Camille wouldn't appreciate him trying to gloss over the seriousness of the situation. He never made inane comments like that with patients and their loved ones, or with his friends and family. It wasn't right to raise unguaranteed hope. Backing away, he returned to looking after Jules.

Camille walked away and quickly returned with Elyna in her arms. 'See you shortly.'

'Hope so.' Then he'd hand over to the paramedics and get on with spending time with Camille and Elyna.

At the end of the day with Elyna tucked up in bed at Etienne's and Louise reading her a story, Camille and Etienne left the house and headed to a restaurant in Versailles with Alain driving. Camille was excited as the restaurant Etienne had chosen had a very good reputation, though she did feel a little underdressed. The dress and jacket she'd bought weren't top of the range. Close, but she hadn't been prepared to spend a few weeks' pay on one outfit. Nor was she used to wearing chic clothes and had surprised herself by feeling she'd like something more special for tonight. Something to do with the way her heart felt about Etienne, perhaps? There was no denying she adored him. It didn't mean she should go OTT in an effort to look appealing though. He'd probably think she was trying to suck up to him even though she had turned down most of his serious offers so far. How much longer could she hold out about moving in with him? It got harder all the time.

Etienne picked up her hand and rubbed his thumb across her palm. 'You look beautiful, Camille. That shade of blue goes perfectly with your blonde hair and blue eyes.'

Did she look unsure of herself? She wasn't used to going on dates recently, and especially to a place like the restaurant Etienne had chosen. 'You're a right charmer,' she said over a dry tongue. She wanted to believe him and yet struggled. From what she'd heard, he'd been out with plenty of stunning women and, while she might scrub up okay, she was not stunning.

'I mean it. Before you ask, I'm not looking to get anything from you.' There was a tightness in his voice that suggested he was annoyed with her response.

She squeezed his hand since he was still holding hers. 'I'm not used to compliments.' Except all the ones she'd received from Benoit. Although she now knew they'd been about getting his own way and making her believe he was one hundred per cent there for her. She should've realised that was a warning sign. Instead she'd been a fool and fallen for everything he'd said. 'I was letting my past get in the way for a moment.'

'That's something I fully understand.' Etienne set her hand back on her thigh. 'Let's relax and enjoy our evening. Put aside the things we both worry about and need to discuss and make the most of wonderful food, wine and company.'

As she said, he was a charmer, but this she would accept. 'Sounds perfect.'

And it was. Much later she placed her fork on the empty plate. 'That meal was beyond anything I've ever eaten. Seriously amazing.'

'Glad you like it. This is one of my favourite restaurants.'

'One of them?' asked a passing waiter. 'We thought it was your only one considering how often we see you.' He grinned.

Etienne laughed. 'You're right, Gabriel. I was downplaying how often I come here. I can't have Camille thinking I don't do any cooking.'

'As I've seen your spotless kitchen, it's hardly a surprise,' she retorted through a smile. 'Plus the fact the staff here seem to know you well.' She was a little surprised the waiter had made a comment as he passed them. She'd thought that would be a complete no-no in such an upmarket restaurant. But this was Etienne and being friendly was his mark.

'Would you like dessert?' he asked. 'Or coffee?'

'Coffee, thanks.' They'd taken a while over the meal and suddenly she felt tiredness creeping in, which wasn't right considering she was out with the man of her dreams. Dreams that weren't going to come true, she reminded herself.

Etienne was watching her as he beckoned Gabriel back and ordered coffees. 'What's up? You suddenly look sad.'

Sad? Yes, that was one word for the heaviness settling in her chest. She had to get over this love for Etienne and focus on just being Elyna's mother whenever she was with him. Except they were on a dinner date. Or had he invited her out just to give her a break from her routine? She needed to put her happy face on or he'd think she wasn't enjoying herself. 'Just a wave of tiredness. Elyna woke me quite often last night. She was very restless.'

'Nothing wrong with her?' he asked instantly.

'No health issues. She's sometimes belligerent when it's bedtime and on those occasions she can continue throughout the night.'

'How do you stay sane and calm at work when that happens?'

With difficulty at times. 'Who says I do? I focus

on why I'm there and do my best to keep Elyna out of my mind.'

'That can't be easy.'

'It's not.'

'Do you have to work as much as you do? I know I've asked before, but if I can help out so you have more time off then please say so.'

Everything came back to what he had and she didn't. Maybe not everything, but enough to suddenly undermine her belief that she was doing a reasonable job as a parent. Wealth didn't answer all life's problems, did it? 'I need to work for my own sake,' she growled, and ignored the twinge of guilt that brought on. Here she was in a top-rated restaurant snapping at Etienne! 'I did mention before how I can't cope being at home all the time, that I also need stimulus through work.'

He reached for her hands. 'Hey, I'm not trying to provoke you. I understand why you want to work. What I was offering was to help by taking away some of the financial burden so that if you want to cut back your hours you can. Not stop work completely.' His thumbs were brushing the backs of her hands, making it impossible to concentrate on anything else.

She had to try. 'I guess I overreact sometimes. But I don't want you thinking I'm out to get whatever I can.' His thumbs were warm and gentle, cranking up her libido too easily. *Pull your hands away.* She remained as she was, soaking up the moment and all the heat and her longing for him swelling inside her.

'Your coffee, Mademoiselle, Monsieur.'

A small cup appeared before her, cutting through the heat filling her and reminding her where she was. It was hard to shift her hands because Etienne was so warm but she managed. 'Thank you.' Was she thanking the waiter or Etienne? What a mess she was making of her life and possibly Elyna's, too. She needed to sort herself out. Now. Pushing the coffee aside, she picked up her purse. 'I've changed my mind. I don't want coffee after all.' She stood up from the table to head for the ladies' room.

'Camille? Are you all right?' Etienne quietly called after her.

Without turning around, she shook her head. Not at all. In the thankfully empty bathroom she stood staring at her image in the mirror. A pale, worried expression came back at her. She looked hollowed out.

She was an idiot. She loved Etienne more than she'd ever have believed possible. There was no getting over it, nor was there anything she could do about it. The love was there, filling her heart, her life. She was not going to tell him. Nor would she give in to his request to move into his house. That would make day-to-day life impossible; she'd lose her sanity having to see him every single day. It was one thing to work with him, but totally different to be in the same home, sharing their daughter's mealtimes and play time. She couldn't do it. Not when he didn't love her. She wasn't angry about that. He'd never indicated he might, nor used love as a reason to get her to marry him or move into his home.

She'd called off their fling when she'd been worried he was coming to mean more to her than she could handle when he had made it plain from the outset that he was only there temporarily, for a good time. Seemed that she hadn't ever stopped falling for him, that her feelings had intensified and now she was lost. Totally in love with Etienne, and unable to follow up if she didn't want her heart broken all over again. This time she knew it would be a whole lot worse, because he was such a genuine, honest man and the father of her daughter.

A waitress appeared at the door. 'Excuse me. Monsieur Laval sent me to find out if you're all right.'

Closing her eyes, Camille drew a breath. Opening them again, she nodded. 'Please tell him I'm fine and I'll be out in a minute.'

Of course he'd be worried that she'd suddenly walked away from their cosy dinner. But if she hadn't left when she did she might've said what was on her mind and that could not happen. Sloshing cold water on her cheeks, she patted them dry with a towel and, drawing herself straight, headed back out to join him.

Etienne watched Camille cross the restaurant. Her body was rigid, her face tight. What was going on? One moment they were sitting there happy and chatting, enjoying the evening, and then suddenly she left him without a word. Now look at her. It was as if she'd received devastating news, but she hadn't. She hadn't touched her phone all night and no one had come to speak to her.

Which meant whatever was causing her trouble rested on him. Had he said something wrong? Something that badly upset her? Nothing came to mind. He'd offered financial assistance, but it wasn't the first time he'd done so and she hadn't got upset last time. As she approached the table he stood up to pull out her chair.

Camille shook her head. 'If you don't mind, I'd like to go.'

'No problem.' There was but he wasn't asking here. 'I'll call Alain to bring the car around.'

'Thank you.'

He took Camille's elbow and led her out to sit on a couch by the entrance, where he phoned Alain before approaching the maître d'. 'Dinner was superb.' No surprise there.

Once in the back of the car, Etienne turned to Camille. 'Are you really all right?' He didn't believe her. Never before had he known her to suddenly go so quiet. Something felt off centre and he needed to get to the bottom of it.

'Etienne, I've had a lovely evening. The meal was wonderful. I like spending time with you.' She paused and swallowed hard. 'It's just that it suddenly felt wrong. The atmosphere was special. Too good.' Another swallow. 'We're Elyna's parents, no more.'

His gut tightened. The trouble with asking Camille personal questions was that she gave direct answers, which were often hard hitting. Of course she was right in this instance. They weren't a couple, yet dinner had been intimate. He reached for her hand, but pulled away fast. Touching her would not help the situation. 'You're right,' he told her firmly. Trying to convince himself? Probably.

Her body sagged a little. It had to be because she was relieved to hear him agree with her. 'Would it be too much to ask if Alain could take me and Elyna back to my apartment after he drops you at home?'

He didn't like that. She'd been going to stay the night. 'Do you really want to wake Elyna up to head across the city at this hour?' Besides, he wanted to spend time with his little girl tomorrow.

Guilt filtered through Camille's face. 'You're right. What was I thinking?' She turned to stare out of the window for a moment before turning back to him. 'You're entitled to spend as much time as you can with Elyna.'

Etienne sighed. He really didn't understand what had brought on her abrupt change of mood but thought he understood how difficult this must be for her. 'It's all right. There are going to be times when one or other of us struggles.'

Alain pulled up at his front entrance.

Glad that the restaurant hadn't been far away and they hadn't had to spend too much time in the back of the car feeling awkward with each other, Etienne got out and went around to open Camille's door. Reaching for her hand, he gently pulled her out to stand beside him. '*Merci, Alain.* See you Monday morning.'

Once inside, Camille headed directly to the bedroom where Elyna was.

Etienne followed her into the room and was surprised to find his mother sitting in the rocking chair. Worry hit. 'Is everything all right?' he whispered.

'Yes, Elyna's fine, just grizzly. She's woken up twice since I put her down so I thought I'd stay with her to see if that helped. Seems like it did.' His mother was also speaking quietly.

Camille went across and leant down to hug her. 'Thank you. You're so special. A lovely grandmother.'

He had to blink. Glancing at his mum, he saw her blinking too. Giving her a smile, he turned to his daughter, and his heart thumped. This truly was his family. The family he'd dreamed of.

'Mama. Want mama.'

'Oh-oh, guess we were too noisy.' He reached over and lifted Elyna up into his arms. 'Come on, sweetheart. Daddy's got a hug for you.'

A tiny fist knocked his chin. 'Dada.' Another tap in the chin. 'Dada.'

A spear to his heart. 'Did you really just call me Dada?' he asked in awe. It was the first time and he was melting inside. Knowing he was her father was huge but hearing Elyna say Dada knocked the floor out from under him. Tears streaked down his face and he couldn't care who saw.

Camille came to stand with them, her arm going around his waist, holding him tight. 'Wow. I'm so happy for you.'

Glancing at her, he found she had as many tears streaming down her cheeks as he did. She meant what she'd said. Not that he'd doubted her. He leaned in and kissed her salty face. 'So am I.'

Whack. Elyna's fist struck his shoulder and he laughed. 'I think we're raising a boxer.' Lifting her up above him, he grinned and blew a kiss at her. 'Hey, my girl. I'd prefer you took up knitting.'

Elyna giggled.

He blew her another kiss.

More giggles, this time Camille adding to them.

Happy families. It was amazing. Looking around, he saw his mother sneaking out of the room, leaving them to this perfect moment. Again his heart melted. His wonderful family had expanded to include Elyna. And Camille. At least in one way or another. That was still to be fully worked out but for now he was so happy he'd let the worries go and make the most of this amazing time.

'You know you're probably waking Elyna up, not quietening her down to go back to sleep?' Camille grinned, all the tension from earlier gone.

He shrugged. 'Who cares?' But he tucked Elyna in against his chest. The giggling stopped as she nestled closer so maybe Camille was wrong and tiredness was taking over.

Camille still had her arm around him so he remained still, not wanting her to move away. Her hand was firm and warm. Her blonde hair fell in waves over his arm. The hip she pressed into his reminded him of lying curled up around her in bed during their fling. Unlike with any other affair he'd had, he hadn't forgotten about their times together.

Camille rubbed Elyna's foot lightly and when she got no reaction, she whispered, 'I think you've charmed her back to sleep.'

'That quickly?'

'Make the most of it. She might wake again later.'

The thing was he didn't want to move. He loved holding Elyna with Camille holding him. But she was right. Elyna needed to get a decent night's sleep.

Within moments they were standing together looking down at their daughter. Etienne felt the tears rising again. Wrapping an arm around Camille, he held her tight. She had brought him this deep happiness. She was turning his life around. Suddenly, holding her wasn't enough. Turning, he pulled her in against his chest, and lowered his mouth to kiss her. And felt a thrill when she kissed him back, slipping her tongue into his hungry mouth, placing her hands on his chest, heating his blood.

It still wasn't enough. But they had to get out of Elyna's room or she'd wake and all would be lost. Sweeping Camille up into his arms, he headed out of the room and along to his bedroom. The whole way Camille placed kisses on his neck, adding to the heat she'd brought on. Keep this up and he wasn't going to be able to take his time making love to her slowly. And slowly was the only way to go, to pleasure Camille until she was crying out for him. He kicked the door shut, mindful that his parents were here, though their room was right at the other end of the house and they wouldn't hear anything. But they were his parents, and some things were best not made obvious.

Laying her on the bed he knelt beside her and kissed her, as deep as possible, tasting, feeling, wondering at the sensations she was kick-firing through his body and soul. He knew nothing but Camille. The heat emanating off her, the need in her eyes, her strength as she wound her legs around him. Her hands working up a storm in his blood as her fingers touched, caressed, pressed into him. He was lost.

Except he wanted Camille to know the same, to feel him deep within her, mentally and physically, to know how much he cared for her. To experience the wonder pouring from him to her. Rolling off her, he began removing her dress, only to have to stop and let her help get it over her head. His breathing stuttered when her lace-covered breasts appeared before him. Leaning in, he licked her nipples through the black fabric. And smiled when she gasped, then cried out. They were together, as one.

Slowly working his way down her body, over her stomach to her sex, he took his time until Camille was shivering with need. Still he didn't stop, tasting, licking, lighting her up, until her hands gripped his head.

'Etienne, I need you. Now. Don't wait any longer,' she begged.

He obliged, diving into her hot body, taking his fill of heat and need as she came fiercely around him. Moments later he followed her into a pleasure-filled oblivion.

CHAPTER NINE

CAMILLE GROANED AS she rolled over. Her body ached in a delicious way. That had been the night to beat all nights with Etienne. The man took over her mind when he made love to her, stopped all thoughts and reasoning, turned her on and let the wonder take over.

As she reached out to the other side of the bed, disappointment rose. He wasn't there. The sheets were cool so he must've got up a while ago. Guess that meant no sex this morning.

She gasped. Of course. Elyna. She'd be awake and wanting food and attention. How had she slept on as though she had no one else to think about? No one had come to tell her Elyna was up, to ask what she ate for breakfast. Or had Etienne seen to Elyna? *He doesn't have to tell you. He's her father. That's what he would do.*

A sense of being overwhelmed gripped her. This was reality. Exactly what she'd hoped for and now it was here she felt she'd lost something precious. She was alone. Etienne had a family to turn to for help. He had asked her to join him permanently and she'd turned him down. Should she change her mind? No. Her heart hurt enough now. Imagine how that would feel living in a marriage without love. Impossible.

She crawled out of bed and went to stand under the shower to wash away the aches that moments ago had felt wonderful. She'd been wrong to make love with Etienne. It wasn't making anything easier. She felt lonelier than ever. Because she knew what it was like to be held in his arms, to touch him and be touched in return.

Back in the bedroom she was relieved to find her bag on a chair. 'Thanks, Etienne,' she muttered. Always thoughtful. Hauling on jeans and a jersey, she headed down the hall to the kitchen dining area. 'Morning, Etienne. Sorry I didn't hear Elyna call out.'

He was sitting at the table doing something on his computer. 'Glad you got some sleep.'

Looking around the room, she couldn't see Elyna, nor hear her. 'Where is she?'

'Gone out with Mum and Dad for breakfast and a trip to the market.'

Leaning against the counter, she crossed her arms under her breasts and breathed deep. This was something she had to get used to. Elyna was part of a bigger family now and decisions weren't always up to her. But, 'Why didn't you wake me?'

'I figured after all last night's activity you'd enjoy a sleep in for once.' He smiled slowly.

'Thank you,' she snapped. 'But I like to know what's going on with Elyna.'

Etienne came across and placed his hands on her shoulders. 'From the moment I got her up she was happy and giggling non-stop. It seemed ideal for her to go out with her grandparents for an hour or two. It's what you've indicated you want for her.'

Of course, he was right. Didn't make her any happier though. 'I suppose.'

His smile dipped, then returned. 'You and I can have breakfast together, maybe talk about what to do with the rest of the day, since I'm going away for a couple of days.'

He sounded so reasonable, yet she felt tense. Everything was going well so why did it feel as though it was all slipping through her fingers? Raising Elyna as she'd done so far was changing too fast for her to keep up.

'Coffee? Bagel?' Etienne asked.

She nodded.

'What's wrong, Camille? Are you having regrets about last night?'

'No, yes. I don't know.' It had been wonderful but she'd crossed the line. Etienne didn't love her, end of. Now he looked as though she'd kicked him in the gut. Well, her gut was aching too. 'We can't have a relationship that's not permanent, and that's not happening.' *Because you don't love me.*

He'd made love to her last night as though he cared deeply for her. But she loved him wholeheartedly. No doubt whatsoever. Therefore it was time to step up and say it as it was. 'Etienne, I care about you a lot. You can trust me to do the right thing for you and Elyna. But that's as far as our relationship goes.'

A punch in the stomach would've been easier to take. The end to what had seemed an idyllic night together. 'I see.' The hell he did, Etienne thought furiously. Here he'd been reveling in the warm feelings their lovemaking had engendered and Camille was saying they couldn't do it again.

'I don't think you do,' she said pointedly. 'We're meant to be talking about how we're going to raise Elyna, not getting carried away in bed.'

She couldn't mean that. Except he knew she did. It wasn't in her to lie. He trusted her that much. That didn't mean he could let go all the restraints around his heart. Too risky by far. Even if Camille could love him, how long would that last? They hadn't spent a lot of time together until now and that wasn't enough to really know what was happening between them. He wouldn't factor in that he was falling in love with her. He daredn't. 'Camille, I'm sorry. I thought you were happy to go to bed with me.'

He saw the pain filling her eyes. 'I was.'

That had to be positive, though maybe not, as she was pulling away from him again. He cared too much for her and that was frightening. He was afraid to tell her how he felt. Silence fell between them.

Finally it was Camille who broke it. 'Etienne, I'm sorry but I can't continue what we started last night. I understand you still have issues accepting any woman might like you for yourself, and not want anything else. The way I see it, you need to move on from those fears or you're never going to know real happiness. You have so much to give. You're kind and caring, gentle and generous. You could have it all if you'd let go of everything holding you back. Be strong and go for what it is you long for.'

True. He should, but he couldn't. It was ingrained in him to look out for his heart. That wasn't going to change overnight. He couldn't do what it took. He'd got closer with Camille than any other woman, even teetered on the brink of taking the final leap, but it seemed it wasn't in him to hand over his heart once and for all. 'You think?'

'I know.' Her gaze locked on him. 'I behaved similarly after my ex, Benoit, hurt me badly. Then I met you.' She paused as though waiting for him to say something.

He didn't.

'I called off our fling because I liked you—a lot. Too much. I knew where that was headed, and I didn't want to be hurt. You have a reputation for not getting involved with the women you date. I've no argument with that. At least you're honest. But I also learned that I could open up my heart again, that it hadn't turned to dust after what Benoit did.'

'I'm happy for you, Camille.'

She turned away, headed for the door. 'I'll grab our things and walk to the market to join the others, then catch a cab home with Elyna.' The door closed quietly behind her.

They might be going to spend quite a bit of time together with Elyna but he'd just lost Camille. He'd never really had her because that was the way he liked it. Used to like it. Now he knew he was wrong, but still couldn't seem to risk telling her. 'Goodbye, Camille,' he said to the empty room. Leaning his head back, he closed his eyes and thought about the future. Or lack of, as Camille would say. It didn't look wonderful from here.

Camille was never going to go away. They had Elyna between them. But after this they'd be strictly parents sharing a role, not lovers or even friends.

So much for avoiding pain. His heart was in tatters.

* * *

Nice turned on a clear blue sky and a warm winter day for the start of the surgeons' two-day conference. Etienne didn't want to go into the room with the crowd of general surgeons all talking at once. He'd much prefer to walk along the beach and soak in the warmth, but that wasn't possible. He had a talk to listen to.

Warmth had been missing in his bones and his heart since yesterday when Camille had spelt out so clearly just how badly he was screwing up his own life. She was right. He was. But admitting it and knowing what to do about it were so far apart he was lost. Even after she'd said she cared about him and that he could trust her, he was struggling to take that last step into what could be a wonderful life. He was afraid.

'There you are, Etienne,' called a familiar voice over the heads of colleagues. 'Over here.' Fillip waved.

Groaning under his breath, Etienne pushed through to reach his pal and give him a rough pat on the back. 'Good to see you.' It had been a while since they'd last caught up. He had yet to tell Fillip he was a father. Not that he'd ever be ready for the jibes and teasing that would follow, but he did want his closest friend to know. 'How've you been?'

Fillip shrugged. 'Same old, same old, as the Brits would say. I'm glad you could make it down here. I hope you're staying on after this is over so we can properly catch up.'

'I'm due back in Paris on Wednesday afternoon.'

'Then we'll have a late night tonight.'

They sat down and spent time swapping news on what they'd been up to over the months since last seeing each other. Etienne decided to avoid the subject of Camille and Elyna—Fillip would be onto that so fast it'd be embarrassing.

'How's Torrie?'

Fillip smiled. 'Pregnant again. We're so excited.'

'Congratulations.' He felt a pang in his chest. He was a father himself now and already being away from Elyna was getting to him. He wanted to cuddle her until she grinned at him. He'd love to see her mother too, cuddle her till she grinned and kissed him. That wasn't happening again.

'What's causing that look of woe?'

A bell rang, and the talking around them subsided in an instant.

Etienne sighed. Saved. He'd been about to blurt out what was going on in his life and now really wasn't the time for that. 'I'm fine,' he said and sat back as the first meeting got under way.

Except he couldn't concentrate. The speaker appeared to have everyone else enthralled about a new surgical technique he was using for removing part of the liver, but not him. Instead

Camille's words about how he needed to be brave if he really wanted to have love and a family in his life were taunting him. She was right. It was up to him to sort himself out. No one else could do it for him.

The room became airless, his chest tight. Looking around, Etienne saw a way out without upsetting too many people and quietly left the table. He couldn't stay here for a moment longer. He needed fresh air and space around him.

At the hotel entrance the doorman nodded. 'Morning, Doctor.'

'Morning,' he replied as he strode outside. Crossing the street, he headed along the Promenade des Anglais, hauling sea air into his lungs. Never before had he known claustrophobia, but now he understood those who did. It flattened him, made him want to be anywhere but stuck inside with all those people. It'd been brought on by the perpetual voice in his head telling him to make up his mind about what he was going to do with his future. Every question, every thought, came back to Camille. He couldn't imagine life without her, even though she wasn't fully in his life at the moment.

Did he want her to be? Yes. No hesitation. He did.

Was he prepared to tell her that he loved her? That she held his heart in her hands? It would be the biggest step to take. The step that would win him everything—or lose it all. A step he had to take.

He walked faster. Camille went with him. Her smile cutting through his mind, warming him throughout. Worrying him throughout. This was crazy. Camille had taken over, filling him with hope and yes, damn it, love. Turning around, he aimed for the hotel. He needed to return to the meeting and get on with what he'd come for— to listen to colleagues talk about improved techniques or incredible cases. To be there when Fillip spoke. To be a general surgeon, not a man who didn't have a clue how to front up to what was tearing him apart.

Somehow he got through the rest of the day and the dinner that followed. If anyone had asked him what he'd learned during the talks he'd have struggled to come up with a reply that made sense but somehow he managed to avoid that snag.

Fillip did mention a couple of things and then shook his head at Etienne's lack of interest. 'Sure there's nothing wrong, my friend?'

There was plenty wrong, but he wasn't about to tell Fillip. 'I'm good.'

So good that when people started leaving for the night, Etienne returned to the promenade and took off his shoes to walk along the sand at the edge of the water. He hadn't heard from Camille since she'd walked out of his house yesterday, not even a text to say Elyna was doing fine. Not that he was surprised. She'd been firm about where they were at with this unusual relationship. But he'd like to hear about Elyna. And to hear Camille's soft, caring voice.

What could he offer Camille except to hurt her by not being able to admit he loved her? She deserved better. How about telling her the truth, saying he loved her and wanted to share their lives? She didn't want the tangible things. She wanted love. His? Did she want what he was afraid to place in her hand and wrap her fingers around—his heart?

If she ever said she loved him, he knew she'd mean it. He was afraid to admit how much that would mean because again he'd be vulnerable. If he told her how he felt there was no going back. Which he wouldn't want to do, but he'd been there once, and he *had* survived the pain and anger brought on by Melina trying every trick in the book to keep him. He was here, thinking about Camille all the time, which showed how much he had moved on.

He stopped to stare out to sea where the moonlight made the water sparkle. Beautiful. Breathtaking. Just like Camille. She was not only beautiful and breath-taking. She was real. She could turn his life around. Face it, she already had. She'd given him a daughter whom he adored. She'd shaken his determination to remain aloof with women. She'd burrowed into his heart and wasn't in a hurry to leave.

He had to talk to her. Now. Which was impossible. They were at opposite ends of the country. He couldn't just drive around the corner to ring the bell at her apartment. Nor was he going to phone her. That wouldn't feel right. He needed to watch her face when he opened up his heart. If she was going to turn her back on him, then he needed to see her do it so he'd know for certain where he stood.

Camille said she'd stopped their fling because she'd begun to like him too much. Hope flared under his ribs. Could she possibly love him? Would she believe he loved her? Was he setting himself up for a big fall? Only one way to find out and the sooner the better for his heart. He had to talk to her. To lay his heart on the line. It wouldn't be easy. Managing to breathe while he waited for her reaction would be difficult. But carrying on living the life he had now would be pathetic. Who knew? As Camille had said, he might be able to have it all.

'I do want it all. More than that, I want to give all I've got in my heart to Camille, and Elyna.'

To hell with the conference. There'd be plenty more of those.

There was only one chance at love. Now all he had to do was convince Camille how much he loved her.

* * *

Camille laid Elyna down for her afternoon nap. Her wee girl was very tired so hopefully she'd soon fall asleep. It had been a couple of days since she'd walked away from Etienne for the second time. The ward had been busier than normal, which helped keep her focused on work. At least Etienne hadn't been there but he'd be back tomorrow. Working together wasn't going to be as comfortable as it used to be.

She'd annoyed him when she'd spoken her mind about letting go of his hang-ups. So what if she'd been out of line? She loved him so much she'd had to try to make him see there was a chance at a wonderful future if he was prepared to take a risk. Of course, that probably wouldn't be with her. More than likely he didn't care for her beyond a friend who happened to be the mother of his child, and went to bed with him too easily. For her, being blunt was the only way to approach him. She was amazed he hadn't done a runner when she'd told him she cared a lot for him. Instead he hadn't acknowledged her declaration. That hurt beyond belief, but she'd known to expect it. He wouldn't leave Elyna though, so their relationship was going to become a strained mess.

Would she ever find a man who loved her? First she had to get over Etienne and that wasn't going to happen overnight. Nor be easy when they'd see so much of each other around Elyna and at work. It might be wise to change her job. Except she enjoyed working on the ward, liked the other staff. But to always be knocking up against Etienne when he filled her heart wasn't on. The future looked lonely. She didn't want much, just Elyna and a man to love and be loved by. Etienne.

Out in the kitchen she turned on the coffee maker. Something to eat would be sensible but her appetite had taken leave over the past two days.

There was a knock on her door. Who could that be? Maree was at the hospital visiting Jules, who was making slow progress after his stroke. Peering through the peephole, she gasped. Etienne. He was meant to be in Nice. What did he want? Was this when they got down to the nitty-gritty of how and where Elyna was raised because she'd walked away from him after an amazing night making love? Only one way to find out and she wasn't going to put it off—even if her heart was going into overdrive with worry.

Wrenching the door wide, she said, 'Hello, Etienne. You're back early.'

He looked terrible, as though he hadn't slept at all. 'Camille, can I come in?'

Stepping back, she nodded. 'Of course. Elyna's only just gone to sleep though.'

'She's not the reason I'm here.'

Closing the door, she led the way to the kitchen. 'Would you like a coffee?'

'Okay.' Etienne stood by the counter, looking around. His back was straight, his shoulders drawn back, but there were shadows under his eyes and his cheeks were pale.

This time she wasn't rushing in to ask what was wrong. He'd come here to see her, so she would wait until he was ready to talk. As long as he didn't take for ever. 'Sit down, Etienne.'

'Camille, I need to tell you something.' He looked very serious.

The most serious she'd ever seen him. What was wrong? Had something awful happened? The cup shook in her hands so she put it down. Coffee would have to wait.

Etienne drew a long breath. Then another.

Camille waited, her heart beating like crazy. What was he about to say? Would it be good or bad?

'You were right. It is time I got on with living, and stopped hiding behind what Melina did.' Another long intake of air. 'You've never treated me in the same way. Never. I've always appreciated that while at the same time looking for hidden trouble.'

She sank onto the nearest stool, putting her clasped hands on the counter in front of her.

'You're nothing but honest. Telling me to get over myself was the right thing to do.'

She waited. There was more to come. She knew it by the tension rippling off him in waves, by the way he was looking at her as if he were about to step into a minefield.

'Camille, I love you. I think I have from the moment you walked away from our fling. Even before then you were in my head all the time, annoying me with the suspicion that you might be the one if I could only stop and take a long look at what I was doing to myself by hanging onto the past so determinedly.'

'You love me?' she croaked over a suddenly dry tongue.

Etienne was in front of her, reaching for her. 'Yes, darling, I do. I love you with all my heart. I'm sorry it's taken a while to tell you but first I had to tell myself.'

She blinked at him, totally lost for words. Etienne loved her. She could see it in his eyes, his face and that delicious smile on those amazing lips. *He loves me*. A solitary tear slipped out of the corner of her right eye and slid slowly down her cheek. 'Phew,' she choked out.

He laughed. 'Is that all you've got to say?'

She nodded. Then proved herself wrong. 'I love you too, Etienne. So much it hurts.'

'I need to kiss away that ache.' And he proceeded to do exactly that. Followed by making passionate love on the nearest couch.

Followed by taking her hands in his. 'Camille,

will you marry me and be with me for the rest of our lives? I promise to always love you and cherish you and be at your side no matter what life throws at us.'

Marry him? Of course she would. It was all she'd wanted—Etienne to love her as she loved him and to have that family together that she'd always dreamed of. 'Try stopping me.' This was so different from the first time he'd asked her. This was real. 'Yes, Etienne, I will marry you. I love you so much. I've loved you since we had our fling.'

'Mama, wake,' shouted Elyna from down the hall.

Etienne swung off the couch and grabbed his pants. 'I'm coming, little one.' Leaning down, he kissed her hard. 'Camille Beauregard, you've made me the happiest man alive.'

Two weeks later Camille did a pirouette in the middle of the lounge in Etienne's beautiful home. *Their* beautiful home. 'Now I feel I'm truly home.'

Etienne laughed. 'More than when you returned to Rue Roy?'

'Yes.' They'd spent the last few hours shifting her few possessions from the apartment to here and setting up Elyna's bedroom with all her books and toys that had finally arrived in the container from Montreal. 'This is beyond anything I'd expected when I returned to Paris and I couldn't be happier. I'm not just talking about living here but living with you. I love you so much, Etienne Laval.'

'I know you do.' He swept her into his arms and kissed her. 'Love you back, Camille. You have changed my life for ever. I couldn't be happier either.'

'Mama, Dada. Look.' Elyna crawled around them waving a colouring book that had been in the container.

'Never a quiet moment with you, is there?' Etienne lifted her up and plonked a tender kiss on her head. 'Have you got some crayons in that box on the table?'

'There should be some,' Camille said. 'Though she's not really up to speed with colouring in yet.'

'Doesn't matter if she's happy.' Etienne sat Elyna in her high chair while Camille found the crayons.

She felt unbelievably good. All her dreams were coming true. Etienne was wonderful. She still had to pinch herself that he loved her. Not that he didn't show it all the time, but she couldn't get her head around the fact he really had moved on from the past. As she had. Passing over the crayons, she stared at her ring finger. No, she stared at the gold ring with a beautiful sapphire and diamonds on each side. Her heart melted for about the third time that day. It was always melting. Etienne did that to her.

He put his arm around her waist, gave her a light squeeze. 'That sapphire matches your eyes perfectly.'

'So you've mentioned.' She grinned.

'You know my mother's already started planning the wedding, don't you?'

'She has mentioned one or two ideas, which I take to mean she wants to organise everything.'

'Don't let her rule it all.'

'You know what? I really don't mind what she does as long as I get some say in the planning.' Basically she wanted a small wedding with family and their closest friends, which for her meant only Liza, and she was happy with that.

'Are we going with the vineyard setting?'

'What do you think?' It suited her, but if Etienne wanted something more formal here in Paris she'd go with it.

'I'm more than happy. I just want to marry you. Have I told you today that I love you, Camille Beauregard soon to be Camille Laval?'

'Maybe. Tell me again to make sure.'

'I love you, Camille.'

Life couldn't get any better.

* * * * *

*If you enjoyed this story, check out
these other great reads from Sue MacKay*

Brooding Vet for the Wallflower
Healing the Single Dad Surgeon
Paramedic's Fling to Forever
Marriage Reunion with the Island Doc

All available now!

Get up to 4 Free Books!

We'll send you 2 free books from each series you try PLUS a free Mystery Gift.

FREE Value Over **$25**

Both the **Harlequin Presents** and **Harlequin Medical Romance** series feature exciting stories of passion and drama.

YES! Please send me 2 FREE novels from Harlequin Presents or Harlequin Medical Romance and my FREE gift (gift is worth about $10 retail). After receiving them, if I don't wish to receive any more books, I can return the shipping statement marked "cancel." If I don't cancel, I will receive 6 brand-new larger-print novels every month and be billed just $7.19 each in the U.S., or $7.99 each in Canada, or 4 brand-new Harlequin Medical Romance Larger-Print books every month and be billed just $7.19 each in the U.S. or $7.99 each in Canada, a savings of 20% off the cover price. It's quite a bargain! Shipping and handling is just 50¢ per book in the U.S. and $1.25 per book in Canada.* I understand that accepting the 2 free books and gift places me under no obligation to buy anything. I can always return a shipment and cancel at any time. The free books and gift are mine to keep no matter what I decide.

Choose one:
- ☐ **Harlequin Presents Larger-Print** (176/376 BPA G36Y)
- ☐ **Harlequin Medical Romance** (171/371 BPA G36Y)
- ☐ **Or Try Both!** (176/376 & 171/371 BPA G36Z)

Name (please print)

Address   Apt. #

City   State/Province   Zip/Postal Code

Email: Please check this box ☐ if you would like to receive newsletters and promotional emails from Harlequin Enterprises ULC and its affiliates. You can unsubscribe anytime.

Mail to the **Harlequin Reader Service:**
IN U.S.A.: P.O. Box 1341, Buffalo, NY 14240-8531
IN CANADA: P.O. Box 603, Fort Erie, Ontario L2A 5X3

Want to explore our other series or interested in ebooks? Visit www.ReaderService.com or call 1-800-873-8635.

---

*Terms and prices subject to change without notice. Prices do not include sales taxes, which will be charged (if applicable) based on your state or country of residence. Canadian residents will be charged applicable taxes. Offer not valid in Quebec. This offer is limited to one order per household. Books received may not be as shown. Not valid for current subscribers to the Harlequin Presents or Harlequin Medical Romance series. All orders subject to approval. Credit or debit balances in a customer's account(s) may be offset by any other outstanding balance owed by or to the customer. Please allow 4 to 6 weeks for delivery. Offer available while quantities last.

Your Privacy—Your information is being collected by Harlequin Enterprises ULC, operating as Harlequin Reader Service. For a complete summary of the information we collect, how we use this information and to whom it is disclosed, please visit our privacy notice located at https://corporate.harlequin.com/privacy-notice. Notice to California Residents – Under California law, you have specific rights to control and access your data. For more information on these rights and how to exercise them, visit https://corporate.harlequin.com/california-privacy. For additional information for residents of other U.S. states that provide their residents with certain rights with respect to personal data, visit https://corporate.harlequin.com/other-state-residents-privacy-rights/.

HPHM25